The Hut in the Tree
in the Woods

The Hut in the Tree in the Woods

Richard M. Siddoway

Bookcraft
Salt Lake City, Utah

All characters in this book are fictitious,
and any resemblance to actual persons,
living or dead, is purely coincidental.

Library of Congress Catalog Card Number 98-74861
ISBN 1-57008-627-3

First Printing, 1999

Printed in the United States of America

To my cousin Bill

Preface

Over thirty years have passed since I first wrote *The Hut in the Tree in the Woods*. My wife and I were teaching school in Chinle, Arizona, in the middle of Navajo land. We lived across the street from the high school and had access to the building in the evenings. As you might imagine, there wasn't much to do in beautiful downtown Chinle after school hours, so I took advantage of the electric typewriter in my office at school.

By the time I had completed the first draft, rewritten sections, revised and retyped the manuscript, I had spent many hours huddled over the typewriter. But by the time the book was finished, so was the school year. We prepared to move back to Salt Lake City.

The manuscript was placed in a cardboard box, which in turn was placed in the bottom of a corrugated packing box. Many other items were placed in the box, topped off with my microscope, which was too big to allow us to close the top of the box completely and seal it with tape. That packing box joined nearly two dozen others that were stacked in our living room.

I picked up the rental truck in Gallup, New Mexico, and drove it to our apartment in Chinle. The next morning we began loading the truck. One of our neighbors, a twelve-year-old boy named Junior, offered to help us load. Carefully we loaded our furniture and the packing boxes. Junior expressed considerable interest in the microscope as he helped us load. Finally, we waved good-bye and started the five-hundred-mile trip to Salt Lake City.

The next afternoon we unloaded the truck at our new home and discovered one of the boxes was missing. As you have undoubtedly guessed, it was the box containing the microscope and the manuscript. Gloom.

Over the years the thoughts of rewriting the book surfaced on occasion. Our children encouraged and then finally demanded that I devote the time to chronicle what it had been like to grow up with Cousin Bill. Their question always has been, "How much of these stories is true?" My response is that while there is a kernel of truth in each of them, time has added its own patina that colors the lens through which I view these tales.

I hope you enjoy *The Hut in the Tree in the Woods*.

Chapter 1

My Uncle Willard used to say he had been President Roosevelt's personal attorney. I believed him for quite some time until one day he confessed that he had been one of several hundred attorneys who helped administer the Roosevelt family's affairs. Uncle Willard had graduated third in his class from George Washington Law School at the height of the Depression and had been hired by a law firm that worked for the Roosevelts. At any rate, he had continued to work in the Washington, D.C., area until near the end of World War II. Following the death of President Roosevelt, my uncle decided to move back home to Salt Lake City.

When Uncle Willard went to work for the Roosevelts, there had been considerable consternation among members of my mother's family, who had long been staunch Republicans. In fact, my grandfather had run as the Republican candidate for governor against Simon Bamberger. My mother never understood how her father lost to a Democrat. Her family rejoiced that my uncle was separating himself now from the Democratic scoundrels in Washington and was returning home.

Uncle Willard flew home to find a place for his family to live. The competition was keen. The war had just ended, and thousands of soldiers were arriving home and looking for houses. My uncle learned through some of the political contacts he had cultivated that a new penitentiary was going to be built and that there was some land for sale near the old prison. No one seemed anxious to build next to a prison, and my uncle was able to buy a building lot for a song. He then located a contractor who agreed to build a house, and flew back to Washington.

Building materials were difficult to acquire just after the war, and my uncle's contractor had several dozen houses to build. All of the other home builders lived in Salt Lake. Uncle Willard lived a continent away. The contractor kept in contact with my uncle by mail. His letters indicated that the construction was under way but a little behind schedule due to the demand for materials. My uncle was reluctant to reveal to any of his family in Salt Lake where he was building his house because it was so close to the prison, so none of his family knew where to go to check on the progress of the house. In fact, the contractor had not even dug a hole for the footings when the summer drew to an end.

My uncle was convinced his family would be moving to Salt Lake before Christmas. He called my mother long distance, a major évent in those days, and asked if my cousin Bill could stay with us for a couple of months until their house was finished. He didn't want Bill to get started in school in Maryland, where they lived, and then have to transfer to Salt Lake schools partway through the year. My mother agreed to let Bill stay with us for a few months. The few months stretched to nearly two years until the house was completed.

My family met Bill at the airport late in August. This gave him immediate celebrity status, since I had never met anyone under twenty years of age who had flown on an airplane. Bill was two years older than I in age, but decades older in experience. He had been raised as an only child by two adults who treated him as if he were an adult. At eight he spoke and acted far beyond his years.

We lived on Roosevelt Avenue on the

east bench of Salt Lake City. When Brigham Young laid out the plan for the city, he divided it into ten-acre blocks. Starting at the southeast corner of Temple Square, he numbered each block east, west, north, or south of that point. We lived about fifteen blocks south of Temple Square and about thirteen blocks east. The Avenues were only five-acre blocks, with an additional street running east and west through the middle of Brigham Young's ten-acre format. At one time Lake Bonneville occupied Salt Lake Valley. Great Salt Lake is the remnant of that lake. Thirteenth East is located on one of the old beaches of Lake Bonneville. Our house on Roosevelt Avenue was built on the hill that several thousand years ago slid beneath the surface of the water just west of Thirteenth East.

Across the street from our house was the woods. At one time a polygamist family had lived in a large home on Thirteenth East. Behind their home they had planted fruit trees and a vegetable garden, as well as a formal garden complete with fountains and statues. There were a number of springs bubbling out of the hill, and the family had captured the water from these and piped it to the fountains or diverted the flow to water their gardens. In the late 1800s the United States government sent federal marshalls into Utah to deal with polygamy. Legend had it that the family who owned the estate fled to Mexico and while there all but one teenaged daughter died. Years later when she returned, the house had suffered from years of vacancy and had to be torn down. She sold the property on Thirteenth East, and three homes and a duplex were built between Roosevelt and Browning Avenues. She left the estate gardens, however, since she felt that children growing up in the city had nowhere to play. The gardens had been untended for many years, the pipes had rusted, and the fountains and pools no longer had water in them. In short, it was a perfect place to play. We called it simply "the woods."

We consisted of my next-door neighbor, Alan; his backdoor neighbor, Ladd; Neil, who lived next to the west side of the woods; and me. We were called "the gang."

Across the street from Alan's house was "the tree." The tree was an enormous maple that had been planted by the original owners of the estate. It guarded the entrance to the woods. About ten feet above the sidewalk was a forked branch on which we built "the hut." The hut was about four feet square and four feet high. It had been built of old boards we had acquired when my father ripped down an old storage shed in our backyard. The hut had a window that looked straight across the street to Alan's front porch and had a trapdoor in the bottom to be used as an emergency escape hatch. We nailed an old piece of rotted rubber hose to the floor of the hut and left it coiled to be dropped down through the trapdoor if we had to evacuate. The hose was so rotten that we picked pieces of it apart with our fingernails while we sat in the hut reading comic books. No one ever tried to slide down the hose, but we all said we had. Basically the hose provided uncomfortable seating in the hut. It was always in the way.

The door to the hut faced the trunk of the tree. To provide access to the hut we nailed a number of slats onto the tree trunk. These slats were of various shapes and thicknesses. They were nailed into place with rusty nails we had reclaimed from the storage shed. When we climbed up the slats they rocked back and forth under our feet. Every member of the gang claimed to have climbed down the slats panther style—that is, head first—but no one ever really did that either.

When Bill arrived on the scene the gang increased to five members. Since Bill was the oldest and the biggest, he became the leader.

Until that moment the gang had largely been involved in playing together in the woods. After that moment Bill took over the informal education of the gang. I am sure, given that boys will be boys, we had been involved in our share of mischief, but all of that escalated during the next two years under the careful training of my cousin Bill.

Chapter 2

How much candy do you guys usually get?" Bill's eyes gleamed as he asked.

"We get a whole bag full. A whole bag!" The bag referred to was a grocery sack, and during Halloween we really did get the sack about half full of treats. Roosevelt "Av" (never Avenue, just Av) was a good place to go trick-or-treating. The houses were close together and the people generous. We used to travel up and down half a dozen streets from Thirteenth to Eleventh East on Halloween night.

"Is that all?" scoffed Bill. "Just a bag?"

"How much do you get?" we challenged.

"I get a whole pillowcase full. And I do it in less than an hour!" It was hard to believe that Bill could really get a whole pillowcase full of candy, but by this time we had learned not to doubt him. With Halloween only two weeks away we decided we needed to take advantage of Bill's superior candy-gathering techniques. As it turned out,

Bill did all of the trick-or-treating for the gang, and we engaged in a more peculiar form of Halloween celebration.

Bill outlined his plan for us a day or two later. It required some preparation. First Bill and I pooled our allowances (we each got a dime a week) and walked down to the Dairy Queen. The DQ, as we called it, was a half dozen blocks away. We bought a malt for fifteen cents. Bill drank the malt, since it was only the cup we needed. We took the cup home and carefully cut the bottom out of it. Then we punched a hole in each side of the cup near the bottom end and found a large nail that we inserted through the holes so that it went across the cup from side to side. The cut-out bottom of the cup rested on the nail, although somewhat precariously. A string was tied to the bottom of the cup (resting on the nail), then to the nail, and finally to the cup itself. The rest of the ball of string was rolled up and stuck in the cup.

A wire had been strung from the window of the hut to the beam running across the front of Alan's front porch on the other side of the street. The slope of Roosevelt Av was such that the wire was well above the heads of any people walking on the sidewalk, as well as the tops of cars driving up and down the road.

My father had given me an electric train for Christmas the year before so he could play with it. One of the cars in the train set was a crane car. It had a little pulley and hook and was supposed to be used to put derailed train cars back on the track. It never worked. We removed the pulley and hook and installed them on the wire. The DQ malt cup was fitted with a harness at the top and hung on the pulley. The string that was tied to the cup was tied to the pulley and brought back up to the hut.

We now had an arrangement that allowed the pulley to go sliding down the wire with the cup attached. When it reached Alan's porch the string pulled the nail out of the cup and the bottom fell out. Then the whole arrangement could be pulled back up the wire to the hut.

Alan's front yard held three great treasures—horse chestnut trees. Alan's mother, Betty (she asked you to call her Betty even if you were only six years old), told us to stay out of the chestnut trees. "You kids will fall and break a leg."

None of us ever broke a leg. None of us stayed out of the chestnut trees either. We had gathered as many horse chestnuts as we could and stored them in the hut. Some of them were still in their spiny green coats, which were fast turning brown. Halloween drew nearer.

As mentioned before, Roosevelt Av was a great place for Halloween. There were no streetlights except at the corners. The street was as dark as the black hole of Calcutta. About six o'clock the trick-or-treaters started their rounds. This Halloween, as soon as the first one showed up on our front porch, I was off. It took a bit of explaining to my mother that I was too big to wear a costume before I joined the rest of the gang in the hut.

A trick-or-treater approached Alan's house. We loaded the DQ cup full of chestnuts. Betty always gave a Snickers candy bar for a treat, and she always dressed up like a witch and scared the little kids when they came to the door. Two small goblins climbed the steps to Betty's front door. "Trick or treat."

Betty opened the door, cackled, and put a candy bar in the outstretched bags. She closed the door. The two trick-or-treaters stepped to the edge of the porch, tried to catch some light from the street lamp half a block away, and began an inventory of their candy to see what Betty had given them. At that moment the chestnut-loaded DQ cup came squeaking down the wire toward our victims. They looked up at the white shape wiggling toward them. *Pow!* The load of chestnuts peppered them. They screamed. They dropped their bags of candy. They ran off into the night. Although Bill may have anticipated this bonus, it was a surprise to the rest of us, but we were happy to pick up the dropped treats. Since I was the smallest, I was sent down from the hut to retrieve the loot. It was hard to carry the bags up the tree trunk, but I managed. Alan had an idea. He sent me home for a ball of string. We opened the trapdoor, and the next bags of candy were pulled up with the twine.

An hour passed and we ran out of ammunition. Alan had another bonus behind his house: poison-berry bushes. Poison berries were juicy white berries that would kill you if you ate them. (Bill forced me to eat several during his stay with us. They tasted terrible.) We scampered down from the hut, bags in hand, and gathered chestnuts and poison berries rapidly. Back in the hut we sorted out our ammunition.

Living in our neighborhood was a boy named Ivan. We never knew his last name, nor did we know exactly where he lived. Ivan just showed up on occasion and wanted to play with us. Ivan was mentally retarded, and although he was about sixteen years of age, mentally he fit in with the rest of us. Ivan was not appreciated by the gang, because whenever he got angry, which was frequently, he held you by the face with one hand and pounded you on the head with his other fist.

And now it was Ivan who next came trick-or-treating at Alan's house.

"Trick or treat!" he boomed out. Betty appeared at the door. After a moment's hesitation she dropped a Snickers bar in Ivan's bag. The door shut. He turned to leave. We let loose the cup full of chestnuts and poison berries. Bull's-eye!

Ivan's mental capacity was such that he did not put together the white object flying through the air and the chestnut-berry barrage that hit him in the face. He thought someone had thrown them at him from the bushes at the side of the front steps. Ivan threw down his bag and began thrashing through the bushes. Alan pulled the cup back to the hut and reloaded.

Ivan finally gave up on the bushes and returned to the front steps to reclaim his candy. Neil turned the cup loose again. A second direct hit! This time Ivan put two and two together and came running to the base of the tree. Bill was the heaviest of the gang to use the slats nailed to the tree trunk. He weighed seventy-five pounds. Ivan topped the scales at well over two hundred. The bottom slat split off beneath his feet.

Ivan stood beneath the hut, shook his fist at us, and muttered, "You guys gotta come down sometime." He sat down on the sidewalk. Neil wanted to top the evening off by dumping the rest of the chestnuts and berries on Ivan. Cooler heads prevailed. We thought Ivan might make it up the tree, steps or no steps. It looked as if it might be a long night.

Now, when I say the gang was in the hut, I exaggerate. Bill was out trick-or-treating for us all. One of the clothing items that was "in" that year was an opera cape. My Aunt Yuri, Bill's mother, had a lovely black velvet opera cape lined in brilliant yellow satin. She had shipped it to us with her winter clothing she wanted stored. Bill found it. He cut the bottom in a lovely bat-wing fashion and shortened it in the process so it hung to his shoe tops. Sometime in the past he had discovered that Press 25 flashbulbs, even though they had a bayonet base, would just fit across a Christmas tree light socket and screw in. He had basted a string of Christmas tree light sockets around the inside of his bat-wing cape. The sockets were then wired to a doorbell push button and a lantern battery he had "borrowed" from a welding shop down the street.

Three blocks away from us was a drugstore. We went there most Saturdays after getting our dime allowance, but Bill made several unscheduled stops and brought back fifteen or twenty dozen flashbulbs. "We are going to test them for the drugstore," he said. We believed him.

The other three members of the gang each had a red metal wagon. The wagons had black metal tongues that were used to steer them. If you rode one of these wagons down Roosevelt Av the steering left much to be desired. As you picked up speed the wagon veered back and forth across the road and generally tipped over. My father bought me a wooden wagon. It was wider and longer than the metal ones and much more stable. Bill fixed up our trick-or-treat bags and put them and the flashbulbs in my wagon.

Bill started down the street. He was dressed in his mother's black velvet cape with the light sockets installed. Bill screwed a half dozen flashbulbs into the sockets. He had taped the doorbell button to his hand and hung the lantern battery on his belt. He approached Mrs. MacElroy's house. She always gave you a popcorn ball for Halloween. Bill thanked her and dropped the popcorn ball into his pillowcase. The pillowcases had been prepared by Bill. He had bent some coat hangers into rough circles and sewn them into the tops of the pillowcases. When the circles were vertical the pillowcases looked like pillowcases; when the circles were turned horizontally the mouths of the pillowcases yawned open wide.

The next house on the street was the Fairbankses'. They too gave you a piece of candy and sent you on your way. The next house was the Greens'. Mrs. Green owned horses and she entered them in horse shows. She had won a lot of silver platters as trophies. On Halloween Mrs. Green brought a silver tray with an assortment of candy to the door. When she opened the door to Bill's "Trick-or-treat," she looked out into the blackness of Roosevelt Av and saw a little Dracula with green face and black cape. Bill took one look at the tray of goodies and flipped back his cape to reveal the yellow satin lining. One push of the button and a half dozen flashbulbs went off in Mrs. Green's face. She was blinded. She screamed. Bill flipped open the pillowcase, grabbed the silver tray, and dumped the candy into the open maw of his sack. Tossing the tray onto the porch, he quickly pulled the wagon down the sidewalk and behind the hedge on the Greens' property line.

Mr. Green came looking but did not find

Bill. After the excitement died down, Bill moved on down the street, accepting the proffered treats and taking advantage of the trays and baskets in the less-traditional manner he had employed already at the Greens'. At length the five pillowcases were filled. Some did not have a large variety, but they were filled. Bill came trudging up Roosevelt Av toward the tree. As he approached he saw Ivan sitting on the ground beneath the hut muttering words that no eight-year-olds should know or hear. Bill pulled the wagon into the woods a hundred feet from Ivan. He crept through the underbrush until he was behind him. Putting his hands around his mouth and making his voice as low as he could, Bill moaned, "IIIIvaaaan!"

Ivan spun around but could see nothing in the blackness of the woods. Bill waited a moment, then crept closer. "IIIIvaaaan." Most of the time Ivan was a little nervous anyway. We had frightened him a number of times with stories about creatures who lived in the woods. Ivan would get nervous enough to tell us to be quiet. Actually in Ivan's terms he would shout, "Shut up!" while holding one of us by the face.

Bill gave Ivan a third moan, and as Ivan turned toward him Bill hit the button and a dozen flashbulbs went off in Ivan's face.

Ivan let out a scream, threw his candy bag in the air, and ran down the street clutching his eyes. He narrowly missed a couple of parked cars and did run into one fire hydrant. We lowered the twine from the hut and pulled the five bags, plus Ivan's, into the hut.

For the next hour we sorted candy. The booty was distributed more or less evenly, although Bill did get an extra portion, since he had done all the work. We gorged ourselves on the choicest morsels, black jelly beans, until I vomited a licorice cascade from the window of the hut.

Five small piles of candy were left in the hut for future consumption. Bill climbed down (feet first, not panther style) and directed the lowering of the pillowcases through the trapdoor to the sidewalk below. Each of the gang took a pillowcase and struggled home.

"Where in the world did you get all of that candy?" my father asked from the comfort of his easy chair as he folded the newspaper he was reading.

Bill and I shrugged our shoulders.

"Well," he said, unfolding the paper, "don't eat it all at once or you'll get sick."

Bill and I hauled the pillowcases up the stairs to the bedroom we shared. A moment later my mother walked through the door. She put both hands on her hips. "What have you two been up to?" The telephone rang downstairs. "Another call." She spun around and then over her shoulder said, "Don't eat that candy!"

Fifteen minutes later we were summoned to our front room. The rest of the gang were there with their parents. My mother tapped her foot on the floor. "And just whose idea was this?" she demanded.

Each of us summoned his courage, stood straight and tall, faced the firing squad, and then in one motion pointed at Bill. Justice was delivered. Our Halloween booty was seized, and within two days Bill was able to sit down without moaning.

Chapter 3

When the federal marshalls came to Utah and began looking actively for polygamist families, the fathers of these families began looking for ways to avoid the marshalls. Although a large percentage of the Mormons never practiced plural marriage, those who did often provided themselves with escape routes in the event the law came to call. The family who had owned the estate we knew as "the woods" was no different. Dug back into the hillside was a tunnel that ran east for about fifty feet, turned north for another fifty feet, and then back east for another twenty feet. The tunnel was shored up with timbers, although it did not have a very high ceiling, perhaps four and a half feet at most. The entrance to the tunnel was hidden in a thicket of wild raspberries. If you entered the tunnel and followed it through its twists and turns, you ended at a concrete wall. The foundation of the duplex occupying the spot where the old estate mansion had stood now blocked the end of the tunnel. Apparently the basement of the polygamists' house had covered over the end of the tunnel with fruit shelves or some other movable door. It probably provided a convenient exit in the event unwelcome guests appeared. We named the tunnel "the lion cave."

When the estate gardens had been in full flower and well tended, a number of statues had been placed in the hedgerows. Someone had tried to save the statues from damage and had hauled them into the tunnel and placed them next to the concrete foundation.

The general rumor among the gang was that the tunnel was a place where criminals had been chained to the wall and left to die. We dared each other to go back into the last room of the lion cave and touch the faces of the criminals. When you made the first turn in the lion cave and started to the north, you entered total blackness. After making the second turn you were in blackness so black that your eyes never got use to it no matter how long you stayed in the cave. When you reached the end of the tunnel and put your hand on one of the marble faces of the statues, you were ready to die on the spot and add one more body to those stored there. It was, of course, considered unfair to take a flashlight with you. All of us did.

Shortly after the Halloween caper, Bill began looking for a three-pound coffee can. Since no one in my family drank coffee, this was a little more difficult than one might think. He scoured the neighborhood trash cans, but still had no luck. On the way to school was a little neighborhood grocery store. We called it "the store." Bill made a visit to the store on the way to school and told me we needed to stop there on the way home.

During recess Bill explained that the man who ran the store was looking for children to play parts in a play he was working on. Bill thought I would be perfect for a part in the play. He told me we were going to drop in on the way home from school so that I could try out for the part. All I had to do was go to the back of the store near the pickle barrel and pretend to throw up. I knew where the pickle barrel was because we used to go there during lunch and buy a big dill pickle for a nickel. We'd stick our hands into the brine and grope for the biggest pickle we could find. Often there was a slight scum on the top of the brine, but no one seemed to mind.

Bill was waiting for me when school got out. "I've already talked to the man at the store and he is expecting us to hurry right over. Now, all you have to do is really act as if you're sick." I nodded and followed Bill across the street.

I was really worried, I think with stage fright, when we reached the store. "What do I do after I pretend to throw up?" I asked Bill.

"Just do your act, then come outside and I'll meet you there."

"How will I know if I get to be in the play?"

"I'll come back later and find out for you," replied Bill.

So into the jaws of death I went. I entered the store and went back to the pickle barrel. The man who ran the store, Mr. Poulsen, followed me back. I reached the pickle barrel, grabbed my stomach, and began to roll on the floor. The floor was covered with sawdust, and I got it all over my clothes as I flopped back and forth. I accompanied this performance with retching sounds. Mr. Poulsen fell to his knees beside me. "What's the matter? Are you sick?" he demanded.

I continued to groan and roll back and forth. The front door opened and closed. I groaned. The front door opened and closed. Finally I decided I had done my best, so I got to my feet, brushed myself off, and started toward the front door.

"Are you okay? Are you feeling better?" I could see the concern in Mr. Poulsen's face.

"I'm okay, I guess. How did I do?"

Mr. Poulsen looked confused. "Do?"

"We'll be back later," I said, and exited. Bill was waiting half a block down the street. He had taken off his jacket and was holding it under his arm. "Aren't you cold?" I asked.

"Nah, it's really too warm today." Bill shivered a little as we walked home but refused to put his jacket back on. Later that night he produced a coffee can.

On Saturday morning Bill made a "lion roarer" out of the coffee can. He punched a hole in the bottom of the can with a nail and threaded a piece of heavy twine through the hole. After tying a good-size knot on the end of the string inside the can, he pulled the string tight against the can bottom. He then tied the free end of the string around a post on our front porch, pulled the string tight, and ran his fingernail down the string. A roar emerged from the can. It sounded great. Bill produced a Popsicle stick from his pocket. When he pulled it down the taut string an even louder roar was produced.

Bill took the lion roarer back into the lion cave and tied the end of the string to one of the support timbers. With the channeling effect of the tunnel walls, the roar was magnificent. Bill sent me to get the rest of the gang.

I assembled Alan, Ladd, and Neil near the wild raspberry patch and told them what Bill told me to tell them. "Bill saw a mountain lion prowling around in the woods last night. I think it's hiding in the lion cave." The three looked suspicious. "Who wants to go into the lion cave with me?"

Alan, Ladd, and Neil were all a year older than I. In fact, I absorbed quite a bit of teasing, good-natured or not, for being the youngest and the littlest member of the gang. So when I offered to go into the tunnel it put considerable pressure on the rest. At length we all agreed to enter the tunnel together. Since the tunnel was not very wide, we had to enter single file. I was selected to lead the way.

Bill had stationed himself around the first bend and heard us enter about sixty feet away. He pulled the string tight and cocked his Popsicle stick.

We approached slowly, groping our way through the dark. The tension mounted. Alan started to giggle. "What are we afraid of? There ain't no mountain lions around here." He was greeted with a chorus of support.

Just then Bill made a preliminary scrape on the string. A gentle roar emerged from the depths of the tunnel. We stopped. Another gentle roar. Dead silence followed from our end of the tunnel. Another purr from Bill's end. "What was that?" whispered Ladd. Silence.

Bill pulled the stick the full length of the string. A beautiful roar sounded. Three members of the gang emerged from the tunnel running full tilt. Wild raspberries can be wicked when approached carefully; when pushed aside during rapid passage they can be downright evil. There were cries and shouts as the three tumbled through. I crept back to the bend in the tunnel and found Bill laughing so hard he was having a hard time catching his breath. "What do we do now?" I asked.

Bill really had no answer for the question. He knew we were going to be in trouble if we walked out of the tunnel and met the three wounded warriors, so we just sat down and waited.

The gang waited for me to join them. I did not. "The lion got him!" cried Neil. "We gotta go get what's left of him outta there."

"Not on your life," said Alan. "I ain't goin' back in there."

At length Alan and Ladd agreed to go tell my mother I had been eaten by a mountain lion. They left on their mission. Neil, making a wiser choice, went home. Bill and I emerged from the lion cave to see my mother running across the street tugging Alan and Ladd with her.

"How come you guys are so chicken?" queried Bill. "We took care of that old lion, all right."

My mother, somewhat used to our peculiar behavior, just shook her head and went home. Bill explained in great detail how he had killed the lion with his bare hands.

Bill's story was so convincing that Alan and Ladd wanted to go see the dead lion. Bill finally agreed, but told them he had better go in first just in case the lion's mate had returned to the den. So Bill entered the lion cave, leaving us to follow a few minutes later. Bill could whistle by putting his two index fingers in his mouth. He gave us the all-clear sign, and we entered the lion cave for the second time that day.

We had almost reached the bend in the cave when a roar shattered our ears, followed quickly by a piercing scream from Bill. Alan and Ladd fell all over each other getting out of the lion cave. Back through the bushes went the two lion hunters.

Bill and I emerged laughing. Alan and Ladd began to smell a rat. We finally confessed and swore the two to secrecy. With flashlight in hand we reentered the lion cave and showed the lion roarer to Alan and Ladd.

When we emerged for a third time from the lion cave, we saw Ivan approaching. Bill seized the opportunity. "Ivan, Ivan," he called, "have you got your BB gun? We have a lion trapped in the tunnel."

Ivan's eyes went wide. "A lion! Where'd it come from?"

"Probably escaped from the zoo. Go get your BB gun," said Bill.

Ivan ran home to get his BB gun. Ivan had gotten the gun for Christmas the year before. It was a Daisy Red Rider. You were supposed to be able to cock the lever on the gun with one hand, but in fact you had to hook the butt of the gun under your knee and pull up with both hands. Ivan was proud of his weapon. He had shot each of us several times with it. Fifteen minutes later he returned, gun in hand.

Bill had taken his position in the tunnel before Ivan reappeared. Alan, Ladd, and I explained to Ivan about the mountain lion in the tunnel. Ivan wanted us to go first, but we convinced him that he should because he was the only one who was armed. He cocked his BB gun. We entered the lion cave.

Bill waited until Ivan was about ten feet from the bend before he pulled the stick down the string. Ivan had been advancing a step at a time with his Red Rider against his shoulder. When the first roar reached his ears, Ivan stopped. "Did you guys hear somethin'?"

"Yeah, maybe the lion is there."

Ivan refused to budge. He was riveted to the spot. Bill pulled the stick down the string. A magnificent roar broke loose. Ivan, in a sudden flash of heroism, lowered the gun, put his hand in front of him, rushed to the bend in the tunnel, turned, lifted the gun, and squeezed off a shot. He hit Bill in the neck. Bill screamed. Ivan screamed. We screamed. Everybody except Bill exited the tunnel posthaste.

Ivan started hopping up and down in excitement. "I killed it! I killed it! I heard it scream! I killed it!" Ivan was beside himself. He was almost ready to reenter the tunnel and claim his prize when Bill stumbled out of the tunnel.

"Where's my lion?" asked Ivan. "I'm gonna take it home."

"It went out the back door," said Bill. "You only wounded it and I had to fight like crazy to keep it from killing me." Bill pointed to the red mark on his neck. "See where it went for my throat?"

Ivan choked back his disappointment and left with his BB gun in tow. Bill explained how Ivan had cheated and not played the game fair. Bill just couldn't believe that one of his schemes had gone the least little bit wrong. When we got home my mother wanted to know if we had seen anyone dumping coffee grounds into her flower bed.

Bill told me I didn't get the part in the play.

Chapter 4

The snow fell early that winter. My father said it looked like a long winter. My mother made a comment about any winter being a long winter when we were taking care of Bill. It had become clear that my Uncle Willard's house would not be finished by Christmas, but by now Bill was firmly entrenched in the third grade at Emerson School. There was no hope of sending him back to Maryland, and my uncle and aunt seemed relieved that he had adjusted so well to the Utah culture. At least they were reluctant to have him come back to Maryland.

Alan lived to the east of us. Mrs. MacElroy lived to the west. She was considered by the gang to be the Wicked Witch of the West. She had silver gray hair hidden under a bandanna most of the time. Mrs. Mac, as we called her, was barely as tall as Bill and as thin as a rail, but she had proclaimed herself the watchdog of the neighborhood. Her little white house and backyard were surrounded by a chain-link fence. The fence began at the front corner of her house and ran to our property line. Since we lived on such a steep hill, there was a retaining wall between our houses. The wall was about four feet high and had the chain-link fence on top of it.

Alan's family had a small fishpond in their backyard fed by a spring. The overflow of the pond fed a small stream that ran down our back property line, then cascaded over a little waterfall under the fence into Mrs. Mac's yard. She had planted a row of evergreen shrubs along the edge of the stream, against her back property line. The chain-link fence ran behind the shrubs. On the west side of her property was another retaining wall between Mrs. Mac's and the Fairbankses' to the west. The chain-link fence ran along the top of that retaining wall and then returned to the corner of her house. Except for her front lawn, Mrs. Mac was protected from the world.

One Saturday morning early in December, we were awakened by noise from Mrs. Mac's backyard. Bill and I slept in an upstairs bedroom, and we could look out our window into her yard. We jumped from our bunk beds and ran to the window. There in the backyard was Mrs. Mac and a deer.

We dressed as quickly as we could and

clomped out into our backyard in our snow-suits and galoshes. The deer was backed up against our retaining wall and fence. Mrs. Mac was advancing toward the deer, waving her arms over her head. Our galoshes crunched in the gravel. The deer turned its head, looked at us, looked at Mrs. Mac, and started running along the fence line toward the back of her property. Mrs. Mac began to chase after the deer. As she approached, the deer ran down the stream until it reached the other corner, where it stopped to wait for Mrs. Mac. As she approached at a quick waddle, waving her arms, the deer ran toward the house.

Bill and I watched as the deer and Mrs. Mac continued a weird square dance around her yard.

This seventy-year-old woman rarely spoke to us boys except to chew us out. As she reached a position in her yard opposite us she stopped. "Poor thing," she said breath-lessly, "jumped over the fence from your place and can't get out."

We looked back across our yard, and sure enough, there were footprints from the deer. We could see them coming down the slope in Alan's backyard and across our yard; and we even saw the place where the deer had landed in the midst of Mrs. Mac's peonies.

"The early winter must have driven them down for food," she continued. "She was browsing on my pfitzers."

Bill began to chuckle. "I wonder what her pfitzers are?" he whispered to me.

Just then the deer made another dash to the southwest corner of the yard. Mrs. Mac waddled wildly after it. On her next round of the yard she called to us. "Will you boys go open the front gate so I can drive this poor thing out?" Bill and I moved to her front yard as quickly as our snowsuits and galoshes would allow. Bill fiddled with the catch on the gate until it finally opened. Just then the deer came bounding down the side of the house straight for Bill and me. Bill let out a scream and tried to move out of the way. The scream had done it; the deer wheeled around and bounded toward the backyard.

"Don't yell!" Mrs. Mac screamed. "You'll frighten the poor dear." The deer bounded away from her. Around and around the yard they went, but the deer never approached the gate. At last Mrs. Mac clomped over to the gate. "You boys are scaring the poor thing. Now, go home and let me get her out of my yard."

Bill and I walked back into our yard and watched Mrs. Mac and the deer run around the yard. "I know how she can get rid of the deer," Bill said. "Remember how Tom Mix headed off that stampede?" Bill and I often attended the Saturday morning serials at the Utah Theatre. We were well versed in Hollywood cowboy lore. "She needs to rope that deer." Bill made his way into our garage and emerged with two lengths of rope, each about twenty feet long. He sat down in the snow and tied a slipknot in the end of each rope. After opening the rope to form a large loop he called over the fence. "Mrs. MacElroy, here's a rope so you can lasso the deer."

Mrs. Mac turned and looked at us as if we had finally done something right. She scooted over to the fence and took the rope. "It's been a long time, boys, but I think I can still throw a loop." Bill took the other rope, and we made our way down to the open gate.

We had never been inside Mrs. Mac's backyard. As we worked our way warily down the east side of her house, the deer suddenly barreled around the back corner and started right for us. We screamed. The deer jolted to a stop, and at that moment Mrs. Mac threw a perfect loop over the deer's head. The deer spun around and ran back into the backyard. Mrs. Mac had tied the other end of the rope around her waist. When the deer hit the end of the rope Mrs.

Mac was launched into the air and landed flat on her stomach in the snow. The deer continued to run, dragging Mrs. Mac after it. Finally the deer came to a stop in the southwest corner of the yard. Mrs. Mac struggled to her feet and tried to untie the rope around her waist. Before she had completed the task the deer sprinted toward the house. Mrs. Mac was spun around, lost her balance, and fell on her back. The deer dragged her across the yard.

Bill's initial burst of laughter suddenly stopped. "She could get hurt," he said, and he clomped toward the deer with the second rope. The deer saw him approaching and jerked Mrs. Mac off her feet for a third time. As the deer ran past Bill he threw the rope in desperation toward it. He missed. The deer ran to a neutral corner, Mrs. Mac staggered to her feet, and Bill closed in on the deer. He began to swing the rope around his head. Mrs. Mac called out, "That's not the way you throw a rope," just as the deer ran across the yard, pulling her down and dragging her behind it yet again.

I heard the sirens approach and saw the policemen run toward the gate where I was standing. "Where's the deer?" one policeman called as he ran toward me. I pointed into the backyard just as the deer and Mrs. Mac lurched and skidded into view. Then the deer suddenly stopped and lowered itself onto the snow. Bill ran toward it and slipped his noose around the deer's neck.

Mrs. Mac untied the rope from around her waist and ordered Bill to get away from the deer. The deer lay panting in the snow. It was still lying there when two men from the Fish and Game Department arrived a few minutes later with a pickup truck.

"It's still alive," said the first Fish and Game man. "We thought we had a dead deer to pick up." He approached the deer warily. "Who got the ropes on her?"

"I did," said Bill proudly. He was still holding on to the other end of the rope he had slipped around the deer's neck. Mrs. Mac remained silent. The Fish and Game man reached down and slipped Bill's rope from the deer. Mrs. Mac's rope had tightened around the deer's neck. As the Fish and Game man loosened it the deer suddenly lurched to its feet and struck out with a front hoof. The Fish and Game man jumped backward, pulling the rope off the deer. The deer ran across the yard as far away from the crowd as it could get. Then it sank down onto the snow again.

"Deer aren't made for pulling," said the second Fish and Game man. "They don't have the right kind of shoulders. I think you've worn her out."

"She jumped the fence," Mrs. Mac started to explain. "I guess she had enough speed coming down the hill to clear it, but she can't get up enough speed in my backyard to jump out. She's been eating my pfitzers."

The Fish and Game men made everyone move out of the backyard. We all moved into our backyard and looked through the fence into Mrs. Mac's. The two Fish and Game men retrieved two long poles from the back of their pickup truck. The poles had loops of rope hanging from one end. The men moved slowly and carefully toward the deer, which was still lying on the snow. As the men approached, the deer lurched to its feet and scampered past them, out the gate, across the street, and into the woods. The Fish and Game men, the policemen, Mrs. Mac, Bill, and I followed. We searched for nearly an hour but never found the deer. Any tracks it might have made were stomped out by the searchers. At length everyone went home.

That afternoon Mrs. Mac made flags out of pieces of red cloth and assorted slats of wood. She wired them to the fence posts, "just to warn the deer." It must have worked. Mrs. Mac did not have any more deer visit her throughout the winter.

At dinner that night Bill explained how he had roped the deer and dragged it to its knees, saving Mrs. MacElroy from certain death. Bill and I always remembered things differently.

Chapter 5

That winter a tragedy struck our family. My Uncle Mel was a newspaper reporter. He had gone up Little Cottonwood Canyon to cover a story and while racing down the canyon road to meet a deadline had lost control of his car and plunged off the road. The car came to rest upside down in a clump of aspen. He was not discovered until the following morning, and as a result of the accident his right leg was amputated just above the knee.

Bill and I were too young to visit him in the hospital, and by the time he had been released Bill had filled my head with vivid descriptions of the accident and the condition of my uncle's leg. When at last he went home my mother asked us if we'd like to go visit him. I was so frightened by Bill's description that at first I refused to go, but my mother convinced me that we all needed to give Uncle Mel and Aunt Ruth our support.

When we arrived at their home my

Uncle Mel was propped up in bed. He was in good spirits, but all the time we talked to him my eyes kept wandering to the blanket where his right leg should have been. The blanket was flat. Bill, with his characteristic tact, said, "Can we see your stump?"

I glanced at my mother. Her face was turning bright red. "Bill," she said firmly, "that's not a proper thing to ask!"

"You don't care, do you, Uncle Mel?" said Bill.

Before my mother could respond, Uncle Mel pulled down the blanket. He was wearing gray pajamas with red stripes. The right leg of the pajamas was folded back and safety-pinned near the waistband. "I don't mind. It's something I've got to get used to," he said. He unpinned the pajama leg and gathered it up onto what remained of his leg. The stump was encased in a white stretch sock.

"Does it hurt?" asked Bill.

"It's still raw on the end, but I'm trying to get used to my artificial leg." Uncle Mel pointed to the closet door. "It's in the closet, Bill. Get it for me, will you? I've named it Oscar."

Bill opened the closet door and there stood my uncle's artificial leg. It was all I wanted to see; I left and went into the living room and talked to my Aunt Ruth. She was playing solitaire on the coffee table. "It's good for you boys to come and cheer Mel up," she said. "He's trying hard to get used to the idea of having to get by with only one . . . you know." I could see tears in my aunt's eyes. I wondered how *she* was getting used to the idea.

My mother and Bill finished their visit with Uncle Mel, and we drove home. "That leg is neat!" exclaimed Bill. "It has a hinge for the knee and a sock and a shoe on it and it's hollow."

"Hollow?" I said.

"Yeah, it keeps the weight down. And it has two holes just below the knee where you can stick your fingers to pull the leg onto the stump. And it has a leather thing at the top with laces so you can tie it on and it won't fall off." Bill had certainly gained more information than I.

When we reached home Bill and I went up to our bedroom. "I wonder what it's like to have just one leg," mused Bill. He bent his right leg and held it in place with his hand, then began hopping all over our room on his left leg.

"What's going on up there?" called my mother from the kitchen, which was directly below our bedroom. "It sounds like a herd of elephants jumping around."

Bill quit hopping. "Boy, I wish I had a wooden leg."

"I don't," I whispered. "I think it looked scary."

Bill raised his eyebrows. "Oh, you do, do you?" He smiled.

My Uncle Mel and Aunt Ruth had never had any children of their own. Since our family lived fairly close to theirs, Bill and I were often invited to spend the night. My aunt had taught us how to play cribbage and canasta, both of which she loved to play. Since my uncle often worked the evening shift, she'd invite us to come over and have dinner with her and play canasta. After my uncle's accident, we had not been invited to dinner for several weeks. Then my uncle went back to work. He had become very proficient with crutches and was trying to get used to Oscar, his artificial leg. One Friday afternoon my aunt called and asked if Bill and I could stay at their house overnight. My mother agreed.

When we arrived, my aunt told us Uncle Mel would be at work until midnight. Bill and I played cribbage while Aunt Ruth fixed dinner. Bill didn't like to play cribbage because I was a pretty good player and sometimes beat him. "Fifteen two, fifteen four, fifteen six and two are eight," I said and put my peg in the final hole. "I win!"

"Stupid game," said Bill. "Just wait until we play canasta." Bill went to the back bedroom where we slept. The bed in which we slept was a four-poster with a canopy over it. It was much bigger than our bunk beds, and had a very soft mattress. I had always liked sleeping in it. It seemed as if it were right out of a fairytale. Then Bill told me the canopy might come loose, fall on us, and smother us while we slept. The bed lost much of its attraction.

After dinner we played canasta until nearly ten o'clock, which was an hour past our bedtime. Aunt Ruth made us brush our teeth and then go climb into the four-poster. She turned out the lights. The only window in the room admitted the headlights from passing cars. They cast strange patterns of light and shadow on the ceiling. Bill reminded me that the canopy might smother us both. I tried to go to sleep, but everything in the room seemed to have taken on an ominous tone. I heard the front door open and close and my aunt greet my uncle. A few minutes later the hall light went out. The house was silent. The cars that passed and cast shadows on the ceiling became fewer. At last I fell asleep.

The next morning Bill explained what had happened next. After making sure I was asleep, he slipped from his side of the bed. Slowly and carefully he made his way down the hall, past the bathroom, and into my uncle and aunt's bedroom. A few minutes later he emerged with my uncle's artificial leg. He quietly made his way back to the bathroom and left Oscar there.

My dad had given our dog a little rubber mouse to play with. If our dog chewed on the mouse it squeaked. The squeaking drove everyone crazy, so the mouse had been thrown away. Bill was one of the first conservationists; he could never allow anything of value to be thrown away. His idea of recycling was to put these treasures in the bottom drawer of his dresser. The mouse had joined many other items of dubious value. Bill had brought the mouse with him to spend the night.

Bill came back to our bedroom, retrieved the mouse and a spool of black thread from his suitcase, and returned to the bathroom. He closed the door and turned on the light. He stuck the mouse into the hole in one side of the leg and tied the black thread around its neck. He took a towel from the towel rack, turned off the light, and opened the bathroom door. Oscar was placed in the middle of the hall. Bill carried the towel back to our bedroom as he unwound the thread down the hallway. He then came to my side of the bed.

"I'm smothering! Help me!" Bill yelled as he threw the towel over my face.

I awoke with what I assumed was the canopy covering me. I screamed. I tore the "canopy" from my face. I ran into the hall-way screaming. A bed lamp came on in my aunt and uncle's bedroom. It illuminated my uncle's leg standing in the hall. I screamed louder. The leg began to move. My aunt ran out of her room. The mouse popped out of the hole and scampered down the hall to-ward my bedroom and Bill's. My aunt screamed. Oscar fell over. I screamed.

Uncle Mel emerged from his bedroom on crutches. Aunt Ruth and I clutched each other and screamed. As we began to calm down we heard Bill's laughter from the bed-room. Uncle Mel hopped down the hallway. Bill's laughter stopped.

A couple of years later, after Bill's house was finished, I was invited to spend the night again at Aunt Ruth and Uncle Mel's. I told my aunt I'd rather sleep on the couch. She understood.

Chapter 6

We had an enormous Philco console radio. It stood nearly four feet high and had ten or twelve bands on it. We were supposed to be able to hear radio programs from all over the world. Only one band worked. We came home from school, picked up a stack of crackers from the kitchen cupboard and a quart of milk from the refrigerator, and headed for the front room. Lying in front of the Philco, we listened to the radio serials every afternoon. Sky King, Superman, the Green Hornet, and the Lone Ranger burst forth in thirty-minute segments every day. These programs filled our otherwise dull afternoons.

Following the serials was a brief news broadcast. As Easter approached, the governor announced an Easter-egg roll in honor of the centennial year of the state of Utah. Actually Utah had been a state only since 1896, but the Mormon pioneers had entered the Salt Lake Valley in 1847. The egg roll was to take place on the sloping lawn in front of the capitol building on the day before Easter. To make the event even more interesting, some of the eggs were to have money inside them. Bill and I conjured up peculiar answers to the question, "How do you put money inside an egg?" We also decided how to spend the money once we figured out a way to get it.

The state capitol was a thirty-minute bicycle ride from our house. It was, however, only a five-minute walk from the bus stop where bus number five let us off in downtown Salt Lake City. We went to the Utah Theatre nearly every Saturday morning for the Mickey Mouse Club cartoon and serial show. The next Saturday we walked up to the state capitol.

The approach to the capitol building was a huge flight of stairs reaching the main floor of the building. Beneath the steps was a tunnel large enough to drive automobiles through. There were doors leading into the basement of the building from the tunnel. On either side of the steps were stone lions. Around the lions were shrubs and flowers planted in front of both ends of the tunnel. Bill discovered that he could hide in the shrubs on one side of the tunnel and I could hide on the other side and we could call to each other through the tunnel. We walked back down capitol hill and caught bus number five to go home.

Bill set our alarm clock for 3:00 A.M. as we went to bed early Friday night. We had told my parents we were going to ride our bicycles to the Easter-egg roll. We had not told them the hour of the night we were leaving. When the alarm clock went off we climbed sleepily out of our beds. It was cold. We dressed and pulled on coats and stocking caps. Mittened hands gripped handlebars as we rode through the darkened streets of Salt Lake to the state capitol building. We parked our bikes in the tunnel and took our places in the shrubs. At the bottom of the lawn in front of the capitol building was a rope stretched between stakes to keep people at the bottom of the slope.

We had been hiding in the shrubs for about half an hour when four men drove up in two trucks. They unloaded sections of metal rain gutter and stretched them out across the top of the hill. Then they unloaded boxes of colored eggs. They began to fill the rain gutters with hard-boiled Easter eggs. The rain gutter was perhaps two hundred feet long, and it held a lot of eggs. They had nearly finished as the sky to the east began to take on a glow. Bill and I sat cross-legged in the bushes watching the preparations. I heard him give a low whistle through the tunnel. I leaned back. "I don't think the ones with money will roll the same as the real eggs," he whispered. "Go for the weird ones."

About five-thirty the men were finished loading the gutters with several thousand eggs. A huge black Cadillac pulled up the drive in front of the steps. We pulled farther back into the bushes. Out stepped an imposing gentleman. "Is everything ready?"

"Yes, sir, Governor. We got 'em ready to roll."

"Well," he replied, "here are the ones with money in them." He opened the trunk of the Cadillac and pulled out a box of about fifty eggs. "They've been blown out and had bills put inside them." Our question about how to put money in eggs was answered. "One of these has a twenty-dollar bill in it. The rest have ones and fives. I suspect they will bring happiness to those little tykes who find one." The governor chuckled and climbed back into his car. All of the eggs were colored blue.

Bill whistled to me. "They're the only blue eggs in the whole bunch! Go for the blue ones. Forget the rest. Just go for those blue ones."

A crowd was beginning to gather at the bottom of the hill. As seven o'clock approached, the numbers swelled to several thousand kids and parents, all milling around outside the roped-off barrier. Promptly at seven o'clock the governor stepped through the front doors of the capitol and picked up a microphone. There was polite applause from the crowd. He began a short speech on the importance of Easter and his need to be re-elected the following November. Bill whistled to me through the tunnel. I leaned back. "Get ready and go for the blue ones." As the governor continued, the noise from the bottom of the hill got louder. At length he finished to scattered applause, and the workmen prepared to dump the rain gutters full of eggs down the hill to the waiting crowd below. Kids dug in their feet and prepared to sprint up the hill. Bill and I prepared to rush out of the bushes.

The gutters tipped, the rope barrier dropped, and the eggs began to roll slowly down the hill. Bill sprang from the bushes and ran for a blue egg. One of the workmen intercepted him and lifted him off the ground. I lurched to my feet and tried to run. Both legs had gone to sleep. I staggered forward and fell on my face. I could see the eggs going farther down the hill and the crowd racing up the hill toward them. I staggered to my feet and tried to run again. Again I pitched into the driveway. I began to cry. I got up and staggered again. The governor saw me. He walked majestically down the steps of the capitol as I staggered and fell, staggered and fell, and staggered again. He reached me and stood me on my feet. I sobbed.

"There, there, little fellow," said the governor, "don't cry. I'm sure we can help a poor little crippled boy like you." He scooped me up in his arms and hugged me. I continued to cry. In fact, my legs were starting to wake up and it felt as if ginger ale were bubbling through them; when the governor hugged me it made my legs hurt like crazy.

He reached into an inside pocket of his coat and took out his wallet. Balancing me on one arm, he extracted a dollar bill. The gentlemen of the press had arrived on the scene, and as the governor handed me the bill the flashbulbs exploded in our faces. The governor smiled and turned toward the photographers, taking the dollar bill back from my grasp and then handing it to me again for another round of flashbulbs. My legs were getting their feeling back in them. He put me down and turned to talk to the press.

I limped back toward the tunnel, dollar bill in hand.

When the commotion began, the workman had put Bill down and he escaped back into the tunnel. I staggered into it and he motioned for me to hurry. We climbed on our bicycles and rode out of the tunnel. No one paid any attention to us as we made our way through the east parking lot of the capitol and turned to pedal home. Bill was infuriated. "I had five of those blue eggs right there when that guy grabbed me. Man, I could have had a fortune." I debated whether to tell Bill about the dollar bill. I couldn't decide whether he would be mad that I had succeeded where he had failed, or whether he would sweet-talk me out of the money.

That evening the *Deseret News* arrived. The front page of the second section showed a picture of the governor holding a poor little crippled boy. The dollar bill was conspicuously placed in the photograph. My mother looked at the picture. "Why, he looks just like you," she said, turning to me.

Bill muscled his way between my mother and me and looked at the picture. "Nah, this kid's a lot taller and his hair's darker."

"I guess you're right," said my mother,

"but at first glance I thought he looked a lot like Dick."

I was glad that picture had been taken. It kept Bill from telling the other kids how I had become crippled and the governor had rescued me. It avoided a lot of kidding. To keep Bill's lips sealed cost only a dollar.

Chapter 7

Nearly every Saturday morning Bill and I rode bus number five downtown to the Utah Theatre to see the Micky Mouse Club. We saw about a dozen cartoons, entered contests sponsored by a local radio station, and watched the serials. The serials were especially interesting because every week the hero or heroine was left in a position from which he or she could not possibly escape. The next week they managed to escape. One way the heroes and heroines escaped death was by the movie changing a little. For example, one week we all watched Tom Mix ride off a mine-train spur track that dumped him over the edge of a cliff. The next week four hundred pairs of eyes were glued on the screen as the next segment of the serial began. There was Tom Mix in the ore car. There was the spur track and the cliff. But lo and behold a switch had been added as well as another track parallel to the face of the cliff. Of course the ore car zipped through the switch and ran along the new track. Four hundred children sprang to their feet and pointed at the screen. "They added a track! They added a track!" The screams were deafening. That was the real fun of the serials.

One week they began to run a Tarzan serial. This was peculiar in itself, since Tarzan movies were not made as serials. However, with judicious cutting and editing they turned a couple of Tarzan movies into a somewhat disjointed approximation of a serial. Bill had never seen a Tarzan movie. When Tarzan came swinging across the screen on his jungle vine, Bill came unhinged. "We could do that in the woods," he whispered none too quietly. "Man, what a great idea! Tarzan ropes!"

Several problems faced placing Tarzan ropes in the woods, the largest being that we had no ropes long enough. As the summer progressed, however, that problem was taken care of. Increased telephone service in Utah as well as more dial telephones meant the telephone company was installing a number of new telephone poles and replacing old ones. A line of telephone poles ran east and west through the middle of the woods. As the poles were replaced, new guy cables were attached to them and to concrete blocks set in the ground. Since no one lived in the woods, it was a logical place to unload spools of cable from which appropriate lengths were cut as needed. The gang had watched as the spools were unloaded from the telephone company truck. They were large enough that it required a small truck-mounted crane to unload them from the bed of the truck. Two metal tripods were erected, and an axle through the middle of the first cable spool rested on them. The spool of cable was larger than any of the gang was tall.

That night Bill rolled over in bed. We had old army-surplus bunk beds that had been unstacked (debunked, my mother said) and placed on either side of our second-story bedroom. We had painted the ceiling dark blue and pasted cutout fluorescent stars on it. For about an hour after we turned out the lights, the stars glowed faintly on the ceiling. I was lying on my back watching them, when Bill whispered, "Did you see that cable? That's gonna be our Tarzan ropes!"

"How are we gonna ever save enough money to buy that wire stuff?" I asked.

"There's gotta be a way," Bill replied. "I'll start working on it tomorrow."

The next afternoon, as we sat in the hut, Bill told the rest of the gang he had contacted the phone company and they didn't care if we took some of the cable. In fact, they had so much left over we were going to do them a service by hauling it away.

After dinner we retrieved a hacksaw from my dad's toolbox and made our way to the west side of the woods near Neil's house where the spool of cable rested on its tripods. The end of the cable had been released from the spool and was lying on the ground. Bill took hold of it and tried to pull the cable loose. He couldn't budge the spool. "It's like a tug-of-war. Come on, guys, give me a hand." We all grabbed hold and with much straining managed to pull about thirty feet of cable off the spool.

Bill attacked the strand with the hacksaw. He sawed for about ten minutes until he was tuckered out and could saw no more. He made a scratch in one strand of the cable. Neil took over and hacked away for a few minutes. The scratch looked a little deeper. Next followed Ladd, Alan, and I, each with five or ten minutes of heavy sawing. As Bill began his second round of sawing, the first wire in the cable parted.

The sun set; dusk darkened into night. My mother called from our front porch that it was time to go to bed. We had cut about halfway through the cable. It was so dark that we couldn't see well enough to continue, and we were all completely fatigued. "Meet first thing in the morning," said Bill. "We need to finish before the phone guys get here."

"But if we're helping them," I said, "why do we have to finish before they get here?"

"They might not have heard about us helping them," replied Bill. "Sometimes these guys don't hear all those things." We dragged off to bed, with a pact to meet near sunrise the next morning. I dropped off immediately.

Suddenly I was being attacked by Bill. "Get up, get up, it's almost daylight!"

I looked at our alarm clock. It was 4:30. "Let me sleep."

Bill persisted, and soon we were back in the woods scraping away at the cable. As Alan arrived on the scene we had cut through two more strands of the infernal steel snake. Ladd staggered in a few minutes later, and he and Alan sawed away with renewed vigor. After an eternity, the cable parted. Bill grabbed one end and started dragging it toward the lion cave. "Let's get it out of sight before the phone guys get here."

We had just finished hiding the cable and were going across the street for breakfast when the khaki green phone truck pulled up. "Hey, let's go see if they know about us getting the extra cable," Ladd suggested.

"Nah, they're too busy right now. I'll go check with them later," replied Bill.

Later that afternoon I asked Bill if he had checked with the telephone workers. He thanked me for reminding him and disappeared into the woods. When he reappeared ten minutes later, he told me he had checked with them and they had cut a bunch of cables for us. "After dinner we'll go get the cables," Bill said.

That evening Bill and I gathered up the gang and went to the spool of cable. There on the ground were six lengths of cable, each about forty feet long. "Wow!" said Alan. "I wonder how they cut through six of them cables in one day." He looked puzzled, obviously remembering our hours of toil.

"They use big snippers," returned Bill.

We grabbed the lengths of cable and dragged them to the lion cave. Bill insisted that we go back with broken tree limbs and sweep the trail we had made through the undergrowth of the woods. As we were sweeping away, Bill returned to the spool and met us at the lion cave with a paper sack full of cable clamps. "We'll need these to hang the Tarzan ropes." None of the rest of us knew what cable clamps were.

"We need four more cables, I figure, to be able to go all the way across the woods," said Bill. "So I hope they leave us that many tomorrow afternoon."

"Why don't we just go tell them we need four more?" I asked.

"They might be different guys tomorrow." And Bill led us home for the night. "I'll go check with the phone guys in the morning. Maybe they will let us have four of the cables."

The next morning the gang crept into the lion cave to check on our cables and clamps. All of them were still there. Bill told us to wait while he checked with the phone guys. Shortly he returned with the news that they were new guys and didn't know we were supposed to have the cables. They were going to check during lunch. Bill told us to meet in the hut after dinner.

That evening the gang gathered in the hut prior to our last excursion to pick up Tarzan ropes. Bill was the last to arrive. He had gone off by himself after dinner. When he climbed into the hut he looked worried. "Those guys still haven't checked. What's worse, they're staying all night!"

"They're doing what!" we exclaimed. Bill explained that these guys hadn't heard we were supposed to take the cable, and they probably wanted to get an early start in the morning, since they were sleeping in sleeping bags around the cut cables.

"We just need four more," said Bill. "I think I know how we can get them."

The other avenue that bordered the woods was Browning Av. Near the edge of the woods on Browning Av was the toadstool. The toadstool was a concrete mushroom about two feet high and three feet wide. There was a piece of pipe running down the center of this concrete chunk. Years before it had been a fountain and water had gushed into the air, splashed down on the toadstool, and cascaded into a reflecting pool around the base of the fountain. The remains of the concrete splash basin could be seen here and there, but the toadstool remained solid as a rock for over three-quarters of a century.

We discovered sometime before that a large firecracker fit down the pipe and a crab apple could be crammed in the end of it. When the firecracker exploded the crab apple flew fifty feet or more into the air. The toadstool seemed to amplify the explosion and it could be heard a block away. We called this activity "booming the toadstool."

My father was a traveling salesman for a plumbing supply house in Salt Lake City. He traveled through Idaho, Montana, and Wyoming. Although Utah had a law banning the sale of firecrackers, Wyoming did not. When my father came home during the summer months he often brought a supply of fireworks from Wyoming for us to use on the Fourth of July. We had stored quite a number of different types in our sock drawers to use for experimental purposes during the rest of the year.

"You run over to the house," Bill said to me, "and get a couple of cherry bombs." Cherry bombs were really powerful firecrackers. "'Cause you're gonna boom the toadstool."

"Why?" I asked.

"Because we gotta make some noise to get those guys away from the Tarzan ropes while we take 'em to the lion cave."

I ran home and came back with a half dozen cherry bombs and a box of kitchen matches. Bill had taken the rest of the gang down through the bushes next to the camping spot where the spool of cable rested. He left Alan, Ladd, and Neil there and returned to the toadstool. "Wait till you hear me hoot like an owl, then boom the toadstool. The rest of us will take care of the cables."

"Why do I have to stay here alone?"

"Because you're the littlest and you can't

pull the cables as fast as the rest of us." This seemed to make sense. "Meet us at the lion cave after you finish here."

Bill left me listening for his hoot in the growing dusk. I twisted two cherry bomb fuses together and slid the firecrackers into the pipe one after another. I could just see the twisted fuses past the top cherry bomb. I moved up into the crab apple trees on the hillside and selected three big apples.

The phone company men were sitting on their sleeping bags playing cards by the light of a kerosene lantern. There were just two of them.

The previous winter, Bill and I had gone to church one Sunday and heard the story of David and Goliath. When the story got to the point where David hit Goliath in the head with a smooth stone slung from his sling-shot, Bill and I began to question whether this story was true or not. We both had sling-shots—at least we thought we did—but when we questioned the Sunday School teacher, she said that the sling David used was different from our flipper crutches. We pushed her to find out what kind of sling-shot David had used. It sounded like his was much more powerful than our flipper crutches. Our Sunday School teacher didn't seem to know.

The next day in school Bill and I went to the library during lunch. The librarian was very helpful, and Bill and I soon had a book describing slingshots quite vividly. That afternoon we asked my mother if we could have the tongues from an old pair of worn-out shoes.

My mother reluctantly let us cut the tongues from the pair of shoes. Bill went to the drugstore after dinner and returned with two pairs of leather shoelaces. We tied the shoelaces to the sides of the shoe tongues. We tied a loop in one of the laces to fit over our ring fingers. The unlooped lace was held between thumb and index finger. A small, smooth stone was placed in the tongue. The whole arrangement was whirled around your head until it was moving at about half the speed of light and then the unlooped lace was released. The stone traveled in a straight line from the point in the circle where it was released. When I tried firing my slingshot, I usually endangered anyone standing anywhere within a circle of thirty feet or so. I never could control the direction of the stone. Bill mastered this weapon quite quickly. He'd go out behind our house and hurl stones at empty soup cans by the hour. He reached a point where he could hit nine out of ten cans from about fifty feet. He also learned that marbles were better projectiles than stones.

Bill left me at the toadstool and rejoined the rest of the gang hiding in the underbrush near the cable spool. "Get ready," he told them, "and when those guys leave, grab a piece of cable, then run to the lion cave." He placed a marble in his slingshot, began swinging it around his head, and hooted like an owl.

At the toadstool I struck a match, lighted the twisted fuses, and crammed the first crab apple into the pipe. I ran, with ears covered. The toadstool erupted in a blaze of flame and sound.

Bill was standing in the shadows whirling his sling. When the sound of the explosion reached his ears he let the marble fly toward the kerosene lantern. The light went out in an explosion of glass. The two card players jumped to their feet. "Somebody's shooting at us!" They started off in the direction of the explosion.

I reloaded the toadstool and set off a second blast before I scurried toward the lion cave. As soon as the telephone men began groping their way through the darkness of the woods, the gang ran to the pieces of cable and started tugging them through the underbrush. They had to double up on each piece of cable to move it, so they had to make two trips to the lion cave. As they approached with the first pieces of cable, I met them. "Come on, help us!" cried Bill. "We gotta get the cable before those guys get back."

We tugged the second pair of cables into the tunnel and ran back with our broken branches to sweep the trail. The only sign of the men was some thrashing in the bushes near the toadstool. After sweeping the trail we went home to bed.

The next morning was Saturday, and we returned to the Utah Theatre for another chapter in the Tarzan serial. Bill suggested we wait a week or two before hanging the Tarzan ropes. Actually nearly a month passed before the telephone men moved on to another location.

Early one morning Bill remembered the cables. Now we faced the next problem: how were we going to get the cables into the trees? Since I was the lightest member of the gang, I was elected to climb as high as I could in the tree at the entrance to the woods. We decided to attach the first cable so that we could swing from the branch on which the hut rested. With a ball of kite twine in my pocket I climbed as high in the tree as I dared. Clinging to the branch for all

I was worth, I held on to the end of the string and dropped the ball to the ground. I fed the free end in my hand over the branch until it reached the ground. Bill attached a length of clothesline rope to one end of the twine and pulled the other end, which pulled the rope over the branch. The cable was attached to the rope, and the gang pulled the cable up to the branch.

I cautiously descended from the branch to the ground. Bill handed me a cable clamp and a wrench. He had me do a dry run of attaching a cable clamp to the cable while we were on the ground. I climbed back up to the branch and cable. The gang dragged the end of the cable over the branch. I wedged myself against the trunk and started to attach a cable clamp. It was much easier on the ground than in the tree, but after much huffing and puffing I did a reasonable job of securing the cable to the branch. Then I descended for the second time.

The cable hung about ten feet above the ground. It was obvious that we could not reach the ground, nor could we pull the cable up to the hut without some additional help. Of course Bill had an answer. He went to our garage and retrieved one of the ropes he had used to rope the deer. Alan had an enormous wooden extension ladder in his garage. It took four of us to carry it across the street. We leaned the ladder against the tree trunk after much exertion and prepared to attach the piece of rope. I climbed back into the tree and started the cable swinging toward the ladder. Back and forth it went until Bill finally caught the end. He formed a loop in the bottom of the cable and attached a second cable clamp. Then he tied one end of the rope to the cable loop.

The rope hung to the ground. We tied a slipknot in the rope about two feet above the ground and cut off the excess rope. Bill climbed up to the hut and dropped the clothesline rope to us. We tied the two ropes together and Bill pulled the loop up to the branch in front of the hut. A decision had to be made: who would be the first to try the Tarzan rope? Tarzan made it look easy, but from our vantage point the ground looked awfully far away. We decided—or, I should say, Bill decided—we would draw straws. He climbed down from the hut and ran home. When he returned he had five broom straws—four long ones and one short one. He turned his back to the rest of us and arranged the straws so that they all projected the same length from his closed hand. I was first to draw.

"You got the short one! Wow! How lucky

can a guy get!" Bill threw the other straws out the window of the hut. "I guess you get to be the first one to swing on the Tarzan rope."

I put my right foot in the loop. I grabbed the rope with a death grip. I hesitated. Bill pushed. I went swinging in a huge arc from the branch in front of the hut, across the clearing below, and into the tree on the other side of the clearing. I stuck out my left foot. I didn't hit hard, just enough to bring me to a stop and start me swinging back. I almost reached the hut before I changed direction and back I went again. It took several seconds to complete one swing. My arms were getting tired. But what was worse, the slipknot had tightened around my foot. Keds were made for running, not protecting a foot from a squeezing slipknot. I tried to drag my left foot and bring me to a stop. However, when my free foot touched the ground it just barely did so, and while it did slow me down a little bit, its major effect was to start me spinning.

I am extremely prone to motion sickness. I don't even like amusement park rides that spin around. My stomach started to heave. I started to scream. The gang, hearing my screams, did what they did best in an emergency—they ran. I finally came to a stop, but the rope continued to twist and spin me. When I put my left toes on the ground, it relieved the weight on the branch, and the rope pulled me up enough that I could not free myself from the boa constrictor that had tightened around my right foot. I was caught and I was sick.

When Bill ran home my mother thought it suspicious that he had come without me. After some questioning, Bill admitted that I was hung in a tree in the woods. My mother came running just in time to see me vomit. In the best traditions of motherhood she helped me free my foot and get home.

The next day the Tarzan rope was modified. The slipknot was replaced with a non-slip knot. Since I had not been killed, the other members of the gang were anxious to try swinging. Alan went first. He weighed a dozen more pounds than I. The branch bent beneath his weight. When he was tired of swinging, he dragged his foot, came to a stop, and gracefully pulled his foot from the loop. Neil, Ladd, and Bill followed. Bill was the heaviest of the five and cleared the ground by only a couple of inches. The branch high in the tree was quite flexible. Following their successful swings I made my second attempt and found that without a trapped foot I could stop and get out of the swing quite well.

During the remainder of the week we became braver and braver. We even talked about putting up a second rope so that we could swing from one to another as we had seen Tarzan do. It was noted, however, that we all hung on to the rope we were using with a grip that would have taken crowbars to pry loose. It was highly unlikely we would voluntarily let go of one rope and transfer to another. The second rope was shelved.

Monday morning arrived. So did Ivan. Ivan had a habit of showing up on Mondays to start our weeks off poorly. He brought his BB gun in case the lions had returned. Bill took one look at the BB gun and smiled as he remembered past experiences. "Hey, Ivan. We have the neatest swing. You wanna try it?" Ivan looked for the swing. We left it tied to the branch in front of the hut when it was not in use. Bill grabbed me. "Go show him how fun it is."

I climbed up the slats to the hut and loosened the swing. Stepping into the loop I grabbed the rope and launched forth from the branch. I traced a magnificent arc across the forest floor. I had become so brave that I considered waving with one hand, but it seemed like too much of a grandstand play, so I just dragged my foot and skidded to a spinning stop. Ivan's eyes grew big as golf balls. "Man! I gotta swing. Let me do it. Okay? Okay?"

Bill shrugged his shoulders. "It's kinda scary." He assessed Ivan's weight and shortened the rope.

"Hey! If a little kid can do it, I can do it."

Bill shrugged again. "If you really want to." He led the fire brigade to Alan's garage to get the ladder. We brought it back. It was much easier to place against the branch with Ivan's help.

Ivan climbed up the ladder and looked into the hut. "Hey. I never been up here before. You guys got a neat hut."

Bill scampered up the ladder after Ivan, pulling the rope with him. "Hold on real tight. We wouldn't want you to get hurt."

Ivan snorted. "I ain't gonna get hurt. Get outta my way." He stuffed his foot into the loop and jumped from the ladder.

The new loop Bill had tied was a slipknot. It tightened around Ivan's foot as the original knot had tightened on mine. The result was the same. Ivan began to spin as he swung. He began to bellow, "Let me go! Let me go!"

My mother heard his screams from across the street. She came to Ivan's aid. Once his foot was free he stumbled, blubbering, from the woods. My mother shook her head. "He's too big a boy for you to be playing with," she admonished us. And then, for the first time, she looked closely at the Tarzan rope. "Where did you boys get this piece of cable?"

"I gotta go home," said Alan.

"Me, too," said Neil.

"Bill," said my mother, "I'm asking you a question. Where did this cable come from?"

Bill shrugged his shoulders. "We just found them," he said.

"Them? More than one?" My mother's eyebrows pulled together. She folded her arms and began to tap her foot in the dirt.

Bill shrugged his shoulders again. "Just kinda lying around," he said, waving his hands slowly in the air.

"Home," said my mother between gritted teeth. She pointed her finger toward our house.

Following interrogation, a khaki-colored truck from the phone company pulled up to the woods. Tarzan had to relocate.

Chapter 8

There were several small streams running across the floor of the woods. They arose from springs emerging from the hillside. Bill had read a book in which springs were referred to as subterranean springs. The name stuck.

One of the great events of the summer was to dam one of the streams and form a small pond. The streams were only two or three inches deep, and the ponds we made tended to be less than six inches deep, but they were fun to wade through and cool your feet. They were also the site of underwater demolition. We had discovered that by dipping the fuses of cherry bombs in melted wax, they would burn underwater. When they were buried in the bottom of the pond they exploded with a great rush of water and mud. Two or three of them with their fuses twisted together really made an explosion to watch.

Deep in her heart Mrs. MacElroy liked kids, or at least she worried about us. Whenever she saw us involved in anything she imagined could cause harm to us or the environment, she'd come at us waving her wooden spoon. Often this happened if we wandered into her front yard near her flower bed. I had been rapped on the head by that spoon once and could testify that it hurt. For all of her seventy years she had strength in those skinny arms. When I saw her coming I ran.

One of her greatest fears was explosives. We never knew why she had this fear. It seemed to go beyond a normal fear of noise. One time she confided to my mother that she had once witnessed a terrible explosion, but revealed no more information than that. My dad supplied us with large numbers of firecrackers. He made Mrs. Mac miserable.

Neil had learned that if an empty tuna fish can was filled with half an inch of water, and an empty baby food can with a firecracker inside was placed upside down in the water, setting off the firecracker would blow the baby food can almost out of sight. The ensuing explosion typically sprayed water all over the place. Whenever we assembled this contraption in the street in front of Mrs. Mac's house, we'd get one good blast before she came running from her house, spoon in hand. The gang would hightail it into the woods for a few minutes before we returned and fired the second salvo.

Some afternoons we could get Mrs. Mac to chase us six or seven times. Nimble though she was, we could outrun her. Even that gets old after an hour or so.

We retired to the woods one afternoon in early July and shoveled dirt across the subterranean spring. The pool filled slowly with water. Bill sent me home for cherry bombs and matches. When I returned I found that Bill had buried a ten-inch piece of pipe in the bottom of the pool. The top of the pipe was just above water level. The pool was filling and would soon pour into the pipe.

"This is gonna be great!" Bill rubbed his hands in glee. "We're gonna shoot water halfway to the treetops."

I brought about a dozen cherry bombs that we had prepared with waxed fuses. As the water began spilling into the pipe, Bill bent the fuse of one cherry bomb into an inverted J and hung it inside the pipe. He struck a match on a rock and lighted the fuse. As it burned over the edge of the pipe, the lighted cherry bomb dropped into the pipe. With the lengthened waxed fuse it took nearly half a minute before the explosion occurred. When it did, a shower of mud, sand, water, and gravel shot out of the pipe and rained down upon us. It was better than we ever hoped.

Bill prepared a second charge and dropped it down the pipe. Apparently the pipe was filling up faster, because underwater the fuses burned more slowly. Over a minute passed before the second eruption of Old Faceful geysered into the air. We began dancing around, singing, "It's raining, it's pouring, the old man is snoring," as the rain fell from the leaves above us. We were so intent on our fun that we neglected to see Mrs. Mac come out of her house and glare over toward the woods.

"Let's try two of them together," said Bill as he began twisting the end of one fuse around the base of the fuse of a second cherry bomb. The whole arrangement hung like two grapes on a long stem. He slipped the bottom cherry bomb into the pipe and lighted the fuse. When he was certain it was going, he dropped the second firecracker into the pipe. The water continued to flow in, taking the bombs to the bottom. We backed up. Suddenly Alan let out a howl. Mrs. Mac and her spoon had connected. We spun around. We ran through the woods toward Browning Av.

The last scene I remember seeing as I glanced back over my shoulder was Mrs. Mac stirring the pool with her wooden spoon. I cleared the woods before I heard the explosion. I whirled around in terror. I knew we had killed Mrs. Mac.

The rest of the gang gathered beneath the crab apple trees. "What are we going to do?" Alan asked. "We'd better go help her."

"At least we ought to call an ambulance," I volunteered.

"Are you guys crazy?" Bill took over as usual. "If we go back there the cops will know we are the guys who did it. And fire-crackers are illegal." His logic won us over.

"What are we gonna do?" I asked.

"Let's go down to school and play on the tricky bars for a while," said Bill. We wandered the four blocks to school and played in the playground until dinnertime. We walked slowly home. As we approached the woods, I had fears we would see a dead body lying beside the stream. I was afraid to look and afraid not to. I looked. There was no dead body. We went home for dinner.

All through the meal I expected my mother to say something about the attempt on Mrs. Mac's life, but the subject never came up. I just knew that my mother knew and that she was waiting for an appropriate moment to bring up the subject. A century later, when we went to bed, nothing had been said.

The next morning dawned bright and clear. After breakfast Bill and I went out on the front sidewalk to build a "Hitler house." Even though the Second World War had been over for two years, we still built Hitler houses. These were houses constructed from newspaper. After we folded and taped the paper into rather intricate structures, we set them on fire by catching the rays of the sun through a magnifying glass and focusing them on the roof. Usually we ended the event by burning the backs of each other's hands with the lens.

"You still got a cherry bomb in your pocket?" Bill asked me. I nodded. "Put it in Hitler's bedroom. This'll be a real special Hitler house." I complied. Hitler's house was just having its roof put on when Mrs. Mac came out of her front door and started weeding the flower patch on the east side of her house.

"We didn't kill her!" I cried in amazement.

Bill dropped the roof and stood up from his crouched position. He looked at Mrs. Mac's bent form and shook his head in unbelief. "It doesn't even look as if we hurt her."

I couldn't tell whether he was pleased or unhappy at that revelation. He bent back down and taped Hitler's roof to the newspaper house. With that task finished, he began focusing the sunlight on the roof of the newspaper castle. The spot of light was so bright that after you looked at it and then looked away, you'd see a dark spot for a long time. Shortly, a brown scorched spot appeared, followed by a black hole and a wisp of smoke. We began to blow on the embers. The roof caught fire. Hitler's house was soon blazing beautifully. The fire crept toward the bedroom wall. Mrs. Mac stood up, sniffed the air, and turned toward us. Hitler's house exploded. Scraps of burning paper flew into the air.

Mrs. Mac pulled her bonnet further down over her eyes. She shook her head slowly in our direction, turned around, and bent to the task of weeding.

Chapter 9

On July 24, 1847, Brigham Young looked out over the Valley of the Great Salt Lake and uttered the prophetic utterance, "This is the right place." Every year on the anniversary of the entrance of those hardy pioneers into the valley a celebration was held.

Actually several celebrations were held. There was the Days of '47 rodeo at the state fairgrounds. There was a parade down Main Street in Salt Lake City. Many local church groups had parades through their neighborhoods. Sugarhouse, the area of Salt Lake near our home, had its own parade this year, the centennial year, 1947. Sugarhouse was named for a project undertaken in 1852 by several members of The Church of Jesus Christ of Latter-day Saints. A French convert, Philip De La Mare, helped bring machinery from France to Utah to manufacture sugar from sugar beets. The equipment finally ended up in the southeast part of Salt Lake City, and the community was thereafter called Sugarhouse.

Many organizations began producing beautifully constructed floats for the occasion. Marching bands were invited, along with fire trucks, horses, and convertible cars to carry the notables of the area. Also invited were any individual entries that attempted to stick to the theme.

Parades are exciting any time, but when individual entries are encouraged and prizes mentioned, they become even more desirable. Bill decided we would enter a theme float. Although Brigham Young preached that it was cheaper to feed the Indians than fight them, Bill decided we would portray a covered wagon being pursued by hostile Indians.

The oversized wooden wagon my father had given me was modified to become a covered wagon. We had a hand drill and some very dull drill bits. In an afternoon of hard labor we managed to drill three holes in each side of the wagon box, one near each end and one in the middle. Bill had been looking for something to make supports for the wagon cover. His first idea was to make them out of wood. However, the thinnest slats we found split when we attempted to bend them into bows to fit across the wagon box.

We next tried finding barrel hoops that were big enough to span the wagon, but came up empty-handed. Our final solution was a peculiar material called plumber's tape. This was a strip of metal about an inch wide that was perforated with holes every inch or so. Plumbers use it to hang pipes from floor joists by bending it into a loop around the pipe and nailing the loose ends to the floor joists. Plumber's tape is not very substantial, but Bill figured a double thickness would fill our needs. We had one minor problem: we had no plumber's tape. We had seen it in our fruit cellar supporting the pipes in our basement, but those pieces were only a foot or two long. Even had we removed them they would not have done the job. What was worse, we did not know where to buy plumber's tape, let alone find any for free.

July 24 was approaching quickly and we had no support for our covered wagon top. Each of the gang had approached his parents about getting some plumber's tape. Each of us had discovered that his parents did not even know what plumber's tape was. Each, that is, except Bill and me. My dad was on the road selling plumbing supplies. That fact escaped us completely. Friday night my dad came home.

At dinner my mom and dad were talking about how far he had traveled and how successful he had been in selling merchandise to the people he served. Bill and I were listening halfheartedly, when Bill heard the word *plumbing* in the conversation. He sat bolt upright in his chair. Bill and I learned not to get involved during these conversations, because my dad usually glared at us when we interrupted. We usually sat there quietly. Bill did the unthinkable. He interrupted. "Did you sell much plumber's tape?"

My father's mouth dropped open. "How do you know about plumber's tape, Bill?"

Bill shrugged. "I thought everybody knew about plumber's tape."

My mother had apparently never heard about plumber's tape, because she asked my dad what it was. He tried to explain but could tell from my mother's blank stare that she just wasn't understanding.

"Don't you have some in your samples?" Bill interrupted a second time.

My father looked at Bill as if, for the first time, he were actually glad to have him living with us. He excused himself from the dinner table and went out to the car. When he returned he had a roll of plumber's tape in hand. He showed it to my mother, who was singularly unimpressed. Bill smiled.

After dinner the roll of tape was placed on the sideboard in the dining room where the dishes and silverware were kept. My father generally forgot to put things away. During the night the plumber's tape disappeared. The next morning my father remembered it and began looking for it. The search was fruitless.

Monday morning my father left for a week on the road. After he left, the roll of tape appeared in the kitchen. My mother couldn't figure where it had come from. Bill asked her, "Do you think we could use a little piece of this?"

"I suppose so, if you don't use very much." We agreed and went out to the shed with the tape. Although it was not very stiff, it was still difficult to cut with our rusty pair of tin snips. At length we cut six pieces of tape from the roll. Each was about five feet long. The roll had fifty feet of tape to begin with. It was somewhat smaller when we returned it to my mother, but she seemed not to notice. The straps were doubled and then bolted to the sides of the wagon bed, forming three hoops that wiggled in the air above the wagon. We had appropriated an old bedsheet that my mother was ripping up and using for rags. Bill turned out to be a fairly able seamstress. He stitched a hem about an inch and a half wide on each end of the sheet. We threaded a rope through the hems. After nailing the sheet to one side of the wagon bed we turned the whole arrangement on that side and pulled the sheet over the hoops to the other side, where we nailed it in place, then cut off the rest of the sheet. The rope-filled hems were now hanging in front of and behind the wagon bed. Bill pushed the material over the ropes until they could be tied, and then we nailed the ropes and sheet to the ends of the wagon. The whole arrangement wobbled dangerously from side to side but did have the rough appearance of a Conestoga wagon.

We had one week until the twenty-fourth of July. We had a covered wagon. We had no horses to pull it. Bill rejected the idea of training the neighborhood dogs in one week. We had something better than dogs; we had Alan and Ladd.

Alan's mother, Betty, was a whiz at making costumes. Not only was she an accomplished seamstress, but she knew how to form papier-mâché into masks. The gang approached her about making two horse heads for Alan and Ladd to wear. She journeyed to our house to look at the wagon, appeared to be somewhat surprised that it looked as good as it did, and agreed to make two masks. It was a rush job. They ended up looking more like donkeys than horses, but they sufficed.

Thursday morning the gang met in the hut to plan the day. "We've got to be spectacular," said Bill, "if we're gonna win a prize. Everybody's gonna put in a float, and we gotta be spectacular if we're gonna catch the judge's eye."

We all agreed. Bill outlined the plan. It was my wagon, so I got to dress like a pioneer and ride in it. I liked that part of the plan. Alan and Ladd in the donkey-horse heads would pull me down the street. Bill and Neil were the spectacular part. Both of them had black hair. They were to dress like Indians in war paint and ride stick horses after us, whooping and hollering. The meeting adjourned. The parade was to take place at noon.

The parade began about a mile from our house, so at eleven o'clock we loaded the wagon with donkey-horse heads, a canteen in case we got thirsty, and Bill's headdress, which he had made from some turkey feathers and an ostrich plume from one of his mother's hats. It did add some flare, if not authenticity. He also put in a mason jar with yellowish fluid in it, some pieces of cloth, and my father's bow. The last items to complete the load were a few arrows, some pieces of wire, and a pair of pliers. The gang started for the parade.

The main parade route in Sugarhouse led south on Eleventh East from Seventeenth South to Twenty-first South and then turned west on Twenty-first South to Seventh East. We appeared on the scene with plenty of time to spare. The canteen was drained by the time we were two blocks from home, so Bill filled it at a service station on Eleventh East. When we arrived at the staging area of the parade, we could see that the competition was going to be stiff. There were many professionally built floats draped in colored bunting and glittering strands of rope. Many of them had people in pioneer costumes riding on them. A number of them had covered wagons. Our little covered wagon started to look shabbier by the minute. Then Bill told us we were not competing with the professionally built floats; we were competing with the children's homemade floats. Ours started looking better again.

About fifteen minutes after we arrived, a man wearing an armband approached us and asked what number entry we were. Apparently we were supposed to have pre-registered our float and been assigned a position. When we said we didn't know our number, the man shook his head, looked at the clipboard he was carrying, and muttered, "Pioneer wagon." He gave us a piece of paper with the number 101 on it and even helped us pin it to the back of our covered wagon.

"Hey, guys, the real judging is done on Twenty-first South, so we'll wait until then to have the real raid on the wagon." Bill had found out about the judging, at least.

At last the floats began to move. We fell into place between two professional floats. One depicted a pioneer family standing on the ridge of a mountain looking down into a valley. The words "THIS IS THE PLACE" were made of gold-covered letters placed on a sky blue background. In front of us we could see the back of a float that was shaped like a huge seagull. It obviously represented the saving of the pioneers from a horde of crickets by an enormous flock of seagulls. Our covered wagon didn't look quite as spectacular as we hoped.

Bill took two of the arrows out of the wagon bed. He wrapped the strips of cloth around them and secured the cloth in place with a piece of wire. Alan and Ladd put the donkey-horse heads on over their own and stepped in front of the wagon. They had to look out through some holes in the necks, and the masks kept turning, so they couldn't see very well. They had to keep putting one hand up to hold their masks while they used the other to pull the stick wired across the tongue of the wagon.

Bill opened the mason jar and dipped the two cloth-wrapped arrows into the yellow liquid. It was kerosene. As he removed the two arrows, Alan and Ladd jerked the wagon as they adjusted their masks, and sloshed kerosene into the bed of the wagon. Bill made a halfhearted attempt to wipe it up with the rest of the rag, but mostly succeeded in simply smearing it around.

Neil and Bill removed the stick horses from the wagon and put their headdresses on. We had lumbered for nearly a block by this time. Bill spotted a garbage can at the side of the road and threw the bottle with the rest of the kerosene into it. He and Neil gave a few spiritless whoops and trotted past our donkey-horses. Bill waved the arrows in his hand, but he had yet to retrieve the bow from the wagon. The parade moved slowly toward the turn onto Twenty-first South.

As we rounded the corner Bill removed the bow from the wagon. It was long enough that it stuck out both front and back. He had worked for some time to get the bow strung, but with it in hand he took on a much more authentic look as an Indian. He dashed off down the row of floats, and when he returned a few minutes later he told us breathlessly that the judges were at the end of the block.

Alan and Ladd had not expected the ninety-degree weather, and they were sweating profusely inside their masks. The sweat ran into their eyes and made it even more miserable. On they went, one hand to the mask, the other to the wagon tongue, bravely spurred on by the promise of the judging and riches less than a block ahead. Bill dropped back to the rear of the wagon. As we approached the judges, he pulled a match from inside his loincloth, struck it on the pavement, and set one of the arrows on fire. There was a spatter of applause from the crowd lining the street. Bill gave a whoop and raced past the wagon, waving the flaming arrow in his hand.

We were in front of the judging stand. Our donkey-horses gave a spurt of energy and began to trot. Neil raced by on his stick horse, hollering to beat the band. Bill circled the wagon, flaming arrow in hand. Suddenly he stopped in front of the judging stand and put the arrow to the bowstring. My dad's bow took nearly forty-five pounds of pull to draw it fully. Bill was able to pull the string back only about six or eight inches. However, he was only about three feet from the wagon when he let fly with the arrow. It pierced the sheet and fell into the bed of the covered wagon.

The spilled, smeared kerosene had soaked into the wood, and now the whole wagon bed began to burn rather brightly. I was sitting in the wagon bed with my feet hanging out the front. Flames sprang up around me. I exited the wagon posthaste.

Bill circled the wagon and lighted his other flaming arrow. The donkey-horses looked back, tried to adjust their masks, and finally realized that my screaming was due to something more than Bill's and Neil's racing around the wagon. Alan and Ladd began to run, dragging the burning wagon after them. Bill let fly with the second flaming arrow. Since he had circled the wagon, he was now facing the judges' stand. He missed the wagon, which was now moving at a pretty good clip past the other floats, and the arrow skipped across the pavement to rest under the judges' stand. This brought an immediate reaction. The judges scrambled to their feet and started stamping on the kerosene-soaked arrow. Thankfully their booth did not catch on fire.

I had escaped in the nick of time. Except

for a singe job on the back of my hair, I escaped without injury. Alan and Ladd were terror-stricken. Their sweat had made the papier-mâché sticky, and the masks were softening and dissolving on their heads and faces. They were having greater difficulty seeing out of the eye holes, and when they were running the masks kept bouncing up and down on their heads anyway. On they ran, dragging the flaming juggernaut behind them.

Bill decided the time to leave was now. He ran back up Twenty-first South past the floats that were following us. Neil followed him in hot pursuit. I stood there bewildered in front of the judges' stand. To my right, Bill and Neil were running east on Twenty-first South; to my left, Alan and Ladd were pulling the burning wagon west. A hand grabbed my arm. "What number was that float!" a man growled at me.

"One hundred one," I stammered.

"You kids ought to be whipped," said one judge. The others nodded in agreement. There wasn't a happy-looking face among the group. One man was shuffling through the papers on his clipboard. At last he stopped. "One hundred one," he said, "belongs to . . ." And he said a name I had never heard before. Apparently there was another covered wagon behind us with no number.

"Okay, get out of here," said the man who was holding me. "We'll get hold of you later."

I decided to follow Bill and Neil, since Alan and Ladd were out of sight and running farther away from home. I didn't catch Bill and Neil until I arrived home. They were in the hut waiting. Alan and Ladd didn't arrive for over an hour. They had bits of papier-mâché stuck to their hair. They did not have the wagon with them. As they climbed into the hut, Bill said, "Well, I told you it had to be spectacular."

None of us answered. We just looked at Bill and his ostrich feather and shook our heads.

Chapter 10

The stream that ran through our backyard was about two feet wide and three inches deep. My mother was quite concerned we would fall into it and drown. None of us ever did, but we did manage to get awfully wet on many occasions.

The stream did provide another bonus, however. We had a garden in our backyard. We also had three fruit trees planted near the stream, which provided water for them. They survived without much effort on our part. In fact, had we given some effort to pest control we might have had good fruit from the trees. As it was, we had wormy apples and small peaches from two of the trees. Only the plum tree provided any kind of crop. The peach and plum trees were planted in a north-south line in the middle of our backyard. The stream ran past the peach tree on the south. August brought a few small peaches from the unpruned, untended branches, but it also brought thunderstorms.

I was never really frightened of electrical storms—I think because I had sat on the covered front porch of my grandparents' house during electrical storms. We hauled out blankets and ate treats while we watched the lightning display over Salt Lake and counted the time between the flash and the thunder to see how far away the lightning was.

Bill was different. His mother had been frightened, for reasons we never discovered, early in life by lightning and thunder. She passed that fear on to Bill. At the first sign of lightning Bill headed for our bedroom, where he climbed into bed and stuffed his pillow around his head. He also made strange whimpering sounds. It was not often that I felt superior to Bill, but in the area of thunderstorms I felt infinitely older and wiser. Then came August of 1947. Perhaps as a preview to one of the worst winters to hit Utah, Mother Nature got off to a good start during the summer.

We were in the vacant lot behind our house digging a pit to catch wild animals, when we saw the clouds begin to build up in the west. They were enormous gray and black mountains in the sky that rolled past us faster than I had ever seen clouds move before. Bill became noticeably nervous as the clouds rolled overhead. We were perhaps a hundred feet from the back door of our house and fifty feet from the peach tree when the first lightning bolt struck. There was no warning, no distant flash to announce the thunderstorm. That bolt hit the peach tree just a few yards from us. I have heard people describe a feeling when a bolt struck nearby. They talk of sparks flying from the ground, of hair standing on end, of their skin crawling. I felt none of that. I just felt my heart drop to the bottom of my shoes. That bolt of lightning was so close and so bright that it hurt my eyes. But the thunderclap that arrived with it hurt my ears a lot worse. I screamed. I ran for the house. Bill stood petrified in the spot where he had been standing prior to the flash and crash. Then as the rain dropped in buckets, he found both voice and legs and ran screaming toward the house.

A second flash and clap occurred as we ran for our bedroom. Bill passed me on the stairs and was in his bed with the pillow around his head before I even reached the bedroom door.

The rain poured for nearly an hour. When the storm ended we went into the front yard. Water cascaded down the gutters, jumped over the culverts beneath the driveway approaches, and flooded yards. I had never seen a storm dump that much water so quickly. My mother had been grocery shopping when the storm began. She waited until the storm was over before venturing home. We regained our composure by that time, but when she arrived we told her about our close call with death. She didn't really seem to believe us until we looked into the backyard. There was the peach tree in pieces. It had literally exploded. All that was left standing was a trunk about three feet high with three branches sticking out at angles from the trunk. Each of these was less than three feet long with tufted ends where the rest of the branch exploded. The backyard was covered with debris from the explosion. Twigs, pieces of wood, and branches were everywhere. My mother became a believer.

We went back to the scene of the explosion. Bill contemplated the remains of the tree. He walked around it and viewed it from every angle. "You know, if we cut off that one branch, the rest of the tree would be shaped like a flipper crutch." Now, the rest of the world would have said "slingshot," but we knew the difference from our research on David and Goliath.

Bill lost no time in raiding my father's

toolbox and returning with a saw. My father threatened to put a padlock on his toolbox to keep his tools in place. He threatened for nearly forty years, but never did get around to putting one on. Bill began to saw off the odd branch. It took more work and time than he expected. At last the two-inch thick branch fell. The result was a flipper crutch with branches forming a Y to the east and west. The flipper crutch was aimed straight through the vacant lot at Emerson Av on the south. We did attack the other two branches and cut them off about two feet from the crotch of the tree just to make the weapon look better.

The next problem was finding something to attach to our flipper crutch. We had all used pieces of inner tube on our handheld models, so a whole inner tube seemed logical. However, an automobile tire tube was just too big to handle. We settled for a bicycle tube. I had tried to learn to ride a bicycle the previous summer. Alan had one about my size and let me practice on it. I kept falling over. I asked my dad to help me learn to ride a bike, but since he was gone during the week with his selling job, he didn't have much time. I think because he felt guilty about it, he bought me a used bike. Since I had not learned to ride it, the bike sat forlornly in the garage next to our house and developed chronic flat tires. We struggled with wrench and screwdriver to finally free the inner tube from the front tire. Back tires are harder to get off because of the coaster brake. We cut the tube in half at the valve stem and returned to the flipper crutch.

Tying the inner tube turned out to be trickier than we thought. We pulled one end of the inner tube around one of the two branches. With the end parallel to the rest of the tube we wrapped twine around both thicknesses of rubber. We repeated the process on the other branch. It took some time to complete this operation. Then the second problem arose. How to pull the tube back.

A strip of inner tube on a handheld flipper crutch is tough enough to pull back, but a whole inner tube is like a band of iron. We placed a small rock against the inner tube. We pulled, we tugged, and when we let go, the rock sailed about three feet in front of the flipper crutch. Bill sat down exhausted and leaned against the plum tree still standing about ten feet behind the flipper crutch. "There's gotta be a better way."

As Bill sat scratching his head, a glint suddenly appeared in his eyes. "A pulley. We'll use a pulley to pull back the tube!"

My father was an inveterate deer hunter. Each fall he hiked the hills in search of the wily buck, and more often than not he was successful. That meant we had to put up with venison for dinner. I have heard many ways to fix venison so that it tastes like something other than venison; none of them has worked. But the deer hunt did mean that we had a pulley arrangement to lift the deer when it was unloaded from the truck. The pulley hung from a projecting piece of the lodgepole of the garage by our home. Of course, it was really two pulleys joined to each other by a piece of rope that ran between the two blocks. The end of the rope was tied to a cleat attached to the side of the shed. Bill loosened the knot and lowered the free-hanging block by feeding several dozen feet of rope through the attached block hanging from the shed.

"Go get Alan's ladder," said Bill. "We're going to have to get that pulley loose."

I hesitated, for I knew that I could not carry Alan's ladder by myself and I was reluctant to have Alan get involved in our fun.

"Go on! Get that ladder!"

"I can't bring it by myself. You come help me."

"Get Alan to help. He's gonna want to help us with our flipper crutch anyway."

And so reluctantly I went to borrow Alan's ladder and his help.

Alan was ready to help once he found out what we were up to. In fact, he almost carried the ladder by himself. We managed to hoist it up to the front of the garage. "Go get that pulley loose," commanded Bill, nodding his head toward the ladder.

I climbed the ladder and worked the pulley loose from the hook that secured it to the lodgepole. It was heavier than I expected, and once I had it loose I dropped it. It narrowly missed hitting Bill, who was standing beneath it supervising the operation. "Hey! What are ya tryin' to do, kill me?"

I climbed back down the ladder. Bill was already gathering the pulleys and tackle. Alan and I helped cart it all to the flipper crutch.

We tied a loop of rope around the plum tree and hooked it to one of the pulley blocks. Bill pulled the other block to the inner tube and hooked it on. As Alan and I started feeding the rope through the arrangement, Bill centered the rope in the pulleys. We pulled and the inner tube began stretching backward toward the plum tree. "I knew it would work, I knew it!" screamed Bill.

As Alan and I continued to tug, Bill jumped up and down and urged us on. All at once the twine slipped on one side of the inner tube and it came snapping backward. It caught Bill across the seat of his pants and knocked him right to the ground. He let out a yell that could have been heard in San Francisco. As Bill was accustomed to doing, he began running around the backyard screaming. He glued both hands to the seat of his pants where the offending inner tube had dealt him a blow and began hopping, skipping, jumping, and screaming all at the same time. Eventually he calmed down.

We reattached the inner tube and tied the twine as tightly as we could. The pulleys were then attached, and we drew back the flipper crutch. Bill stood a respectful distance to the side. A new problem arose: how were we to let go? Bill suggested, "Just let go of the rope." When we did, the friction through the pulleys let the inner tube glide back to its resting point with about as much kick as a crippled hummingbird. Bill sat down beneath the plum tree and thought.

At length he came up with a solution. He'd drive a stick into the ground to act as a trigger. Bill's idea was to pull back the inner tube with the pulley system, then drive the stick into the ground inside the inner tube. The pulley system would then be released, and the stick would hold the rubber band in place. When we were ready to fire, the stick would be knocked down with a baseball bat.

We hooked up the pulley system again and began dragging the twenty-two miles of rope through it. At last it was drawn, and Bill drove a stake into the ground. The stake was a piece of the exploded peach tree and was about half an inch in diameter and two feet long. He managed to drive it into the ground about an inch and a half. While Bill hung on to the top of the stick, Alan and I released the rope slowly. All went well until Alan started to wiggle the pulley attached to the inner tube in an effort to free it. Bill began to lose his grip on the trigger, and as Alan freed the pulley, Bill felt the stick slip from his grasp as the tube snapped forward. Unfortunately it had nothing loaded in it. But it did snap forward with quite a force. Bill was left with scraped fingers from the trigger's flipping forward out of his hands. "It worked!" he screamed.

Alan and I were not too convinced that this was the way to go, but Bill insisted we load a missile and try it again. The vacant lot behind our house was full of prime dirt clods. Over to the vacant lot we went, grabbed a handful of African sword grass, and pulled it up—roots, dirt, and all. Bill then discovered our next problem: there was nothing to put the dirt clod in to launch it. Our handheld flipper crutches had a piece of leather tied between the two elastic bands; our inner tube had nothing.

We had an old piece of canvas in the garage. It was used to cover loads of trash when we made our annual pilgrimage to the city dump to celebrate the rites of spring. Bill chopped a piece of canvas about two feet square from the tarp. We untied one end of the inner tube, slit the canvas on two edges, and slipped it over the inner tube. The top and bottom of the canvas flapped briskly in the breeze. We then reattached the tube to the arm of the flipper crutch.

The pulley was reattached, the dirt clod placed in a strategic position on the ground near the trigger, and the trigger readied. Alan and I began to feed the fifty miles of rope through the pulley blocks. When the weapon was drawn, Bill drove the trigger into the ground. We released the pulley while Bill held on bravely to the top of the trigger. Alan freed the pulley and I placed the dirt clod in place. It promptly fell from the canvas pocket to the ground. Bill reached through the inner tube loop to retrieve the dirt clod. The trigger slipped from the grasp of his other hand. The canvas caught him in the armpit. He was thrown forward upside down into the crotch of the tree. He screamed.

After completing his second dance of the day around the backyard, Bill sat down and tried to figure out a better triggering system. He kept rubbing his cheek where the skin had been wounded by the tree bark. He muttered and muttered, and finally said, "I've got it. We won't use the stick as a trigger; we'll just tie the pulley on to the inner tube with a piece of string. When we want to fire our cannon, we can cut the string."

We tied a piece of string around the canvas–inner tube arrangement and formed a loop. We inserted the pulley arrangement and hooked it to the loop of string. Alan and I fed the hundred miles of rope through the blocks and pulled the flipper crutch back. When it was drawn fully, Bill tied the free end of the rope around the plum tree. The canvas now looked something like a bow tie. It did not seem likely that the dirt clod would stay in the pocket. Bill hung the dirt clod by the grass in front of the canvas. He rummaged in his pocket for his pocketknife. Finding it, he threw it to me and ordered me to open the blade for him. I complied. Handing the knife back to Bill, I jumped back out of the way. There stood Bill with the dirt clod hanging like a shrunken head by its hair in front of the stretched rubber band. He drew his knife blade across the restraining loop of twine, and the flipper crutch launched its first missile. The dirt clod was ripped from Bill's grasp and sent flying into the vacant lot. It traveled about thirty feet before hitting the ground in a magnificent explosion of dirt and dust. We cheered. Bill shook his hand up and down. The grass being pulled from his grasp had made a number of tiny cuts in the palm of his hand.

"The problem is that darn canvas," said Bill after he quit screaming and dancing. "We gotta come up with something better." After some deliberation we began looking through the garage. We rejected an old license plate and an empty paint can, and then settled on a slightly rusty dog dish. The dish was about ten inches across and had handles on each side. It looked like a shallow pot. Back to the flipper crutch we went. The inner tube was freed from one side arm, the canvas removed, and then the tube fed through the handle on one side of the dog dish, across the bottom, and through the handle on the other side. We reattached the inner tube. The dish hung upside down from the rubber band.

We attached the pulley system, and Alan and I drew the thousand miles of rope through it. While we were engaged in this task, Bill selected a prime dirt clod. He returned in time to tie the rope off to the plum tree. The dirt clod was loaded into the dog dish. Bill lifted the bottom so that it faced forward, and cut the loop of string. The whole arrangement flew forward. The dirt clod launched from the dog dish and traveled almost to Emerson Av before it landed on the sidewalk. We cheered. "If we had aimed it a little bit higher we could have bombed a car on Emerson," said Bill. "Let's try again."

While he selected dirt clods, Alan and I pulled the ten thousand miles of rope through the pulley system. Bill returned to tie off the rope. He loaded the dirt clod into the dog dish. He aimed the dog dish at a steeper angle. He cut the string. Launch two approximated launch one, except the dog dish flipped around and launched the dirt clod into the ground about ten feet in front of the flipper crutch. We didn't cheer.

"We've got to keep that dish aimed right," said Bill. He sat down and began to ponder. He rubbed his bruised cheek and winced. "I think if we hook the string to the dish instead of the inner tube, it will hold it in position." Bill went to my father's toolbox and returned with nail and hammer. After two holes had been punched in the bottom of the dish, it was fairly useless as a water dish but did provide a place to attach the loop of string. We didn't own a dog anyway.

We attached the pulley system and pulled the hundred thousand miles of rope through again. Bill tied off the rope and loaded a dirt clod. The dog dish was aimed straight toward Emerson Av. The string was cut. The dirt clod flew through the air and landed against the wall on the other side of Emerson Av. Success! We cheered!

Bill quickly ran into the vacant lot to bring back more ammunition. Alan and I busied ourselves pulling the pulley system to the ready. Bill returned to tie off the rope. He loaded a missile. We cut the string. The dirt clod swished through the air and landed in the middle of Emerson Av.

"Our big problem," suggested Bill, "is knowing when a car is coming. We can't just keep shooting dirt bombs and hope a car drives by." He was determined to hit a car, now that our cannon was built. We faced the age-old problem of the duck hunter, getting the proper lead on our prey. "I've got it," Bill exclaimed. "I'll go over on the sidewalk and signal you guys when to cut the string."

Bill helped tie off the rope and then ran through the vacant lot to the sidewalk on our side of Emerson Av. We loaded the dog dish with a prime dirt clod and waited. Alan had Bill's knife in hand poised above the string trigger. No cars came. Emerson Av was not a very busy street. We waited. No cars came. Bill sat down on the sidewalk with his feet in the gutter. We waited. Suddenly Bill stood up. "There's one coming. Get ready, guys!" he screamed to us. Bill raised his arm. Alan poised the knife over the string. I waited with anticipation. Bill dropped his arm.

Alan cut the string and the dirt clod flew through the air. Bill was facing the street, watching for the impact of bomb against target. The dirt clod hit him squarely in the middle of his back. Bill staggered forward from the impact and stepped into the street. The driver of the car honked his horn and shook his fist at Bill.

Bill came back to the flipper crutch. He took his knife from Alan and cut the twine holding the inner tube on the supporting branches. He didn't say a word as we hauled the pulleys back to the garage and climbed the ladder to reinstall them on the lodgepole.

That night as we were lying in our beds, Bill turned to me and said, "Let's cut that peach tree stump down tomorrow. Okay?"

"Good night, Bill."

Chapter 11

_____

August ended and school began. We attended Emerson School, about half a mile from our house. I was supposed to be in the second grade, but because my mother had taught me to read before I started school, I had begun school in the second grade and was now in the third. That put me one grade behind Bill, and made me the smallest boy in my class. I endured considerable teasing.

Emerson School was bounded on the west by McClelland Street. On McClelland was the "lunch store." The lunch store was a little place where the schoolkids often went to buy penny candy during lunch. Inside the building was a set of glass-front display cases filled with candy that cost one for a penny or two for a penny. We used to buy mostly the licorice fish at two for a penny.

The focal point of the lunch store, however, was the pickle barrel. There was, near the back of the room, a fifty-gallon wooden barrel. This barrel, filled with brine, held enormous dill pickles. They cost a nickel each. There was a wooden top on the barrel, which was hinged in the middle. There was also a long-handled fork with a leather thong through the handle hanging on the side of the barrel. Ostensibly this fork was used to spear pickles. It may have been used for that purpose when adults came into the lunch store, but when the schoolkids invaded during lunch hour, no one thought to use the fork. We just reached into the barrel and grabbed a pickle. Actually we felt around until we got the biggest dill pickle; then we pulled it out, marched to the front counter near the penny candy display, and put our nickel on the counter.

Once you were outside you could lick the brine from your hand and wrist. Then you ate your dill pickle. There are those who would think this an unsanitary situation, but I am confident to this day that the brine killed any bacteria we introduced. The only noticeable change in the barrel was the formation of a scum on top of the brine, but the first person reaching for a pickle broke that up. And the licking of one's own arm restricted the intake of body filth to one's own body.

The owner of the lunch store replenished the barrel every week with pickles he obtained from some unknown source. Mondays the brine was near the top of the barrel. By Friday both the pickles and the brine had dropped to near the halfway mark. This made obtaining Friday pickles a little hazardous. Usually there was a three-step stool near the pickle barrel. On Fridays you had to climb up on the stool and reach into the brine to retrieve a pickle.

We often asked that our dime allowance on Monday be given to us as two nickels. We discussed which days of the week to spend our money on pickles. I held to the theory that Monday was a good day because the barrel was full and you could feel around for a big pickle. Bill was of the opinion that Mondays were always the busiest days for the lunch store, and so you had to wait the longest to get a hand into the barrel and thus could not reach around as long. He felt that later in the week the lines were shorter and the bigger pickles had sunk to the bottom. I opted for a Monday and Wednesday pickle purchase; Bill held out for Thursdays and Fridays.

Our discussions really became heated as we pushed for our different points of view, but they really didn't amount to anything, since we were always anxious to spend our allowances as soon as possible. That meant we visited the pickle barrel on Monday and Tuesday each week.

One afternoon as we were walking home from school we took the shortcut. The shortcut was a dirt alley running up the middle of the block between backyards. These alleys were used to give garbage trucks access to backyards on both sides and keep garbage cans off the streets. We were kicking a rock back and forth between us, when Bill spotted a shiny object in the dirt. He bent over and picked up a quarter. We were awestruck by our newfound wealth. Bill plunged it deep into his pants pocket and started dreaming out loud of all the things he was going to buy with that quarter. I tried to convince him we should share, since we were both there when he found it. Bill was unwavering. He found it; he'd spend it. I grumbled a little, but Bill continued to voice his dreams. I became caught up in what he was going to buy with his quarter.

It was Friday and we had the whole weekend to consider the possibilities; and we would have the bonus of our allowances on Monday. As we walked to school on Monday, Bill began the usual argument about pickle buying, when it hit him. He had enough to buy a pickle every day of the week, with a dime to spare. In an uncharacteristic gesture he handed me the two nickels of his allowance and told me it was my part of the find.

At morning recess Bill announced his intentions. There was no need to argue about which day of the week to buy pickles; he would purchase one every lunch that whole week. I realized that I, too, could purchase four pickles. I decided to skip Wednesday.

During lunch I kept looking at Bill and asking when we were going to buy our pickles. He kept his eye on the doorway of the lunch store, and when the line finally made it inside, he stood up, folded our brown paper bags so they could be taken home and used again, and stuffed them in his belt. "Let's go. The line has gone down."

We made our way to the lunch store and pulled open the screen door. The line to the pickle barrel was about twenty kids deep. We finally reached the barrel and plunged in our hands, and felt for the biggest pickles. After retrieving our prizes we walked to the front counter. I put my nickel there. Bill put his quarter on the counter. A silence fell over the crowd. No one there got a quarter for an allowance. Bill waited for his change and nonchalantly thrust the two dimes into his pocket. He fairly swaggered as he walked out the door. We walked across the street and sat down under a tree to eat our pickles.

On the way home the rest of the gang joined us. "Where'd ya get a quarter, Bill?" asked Neil. "Did ya hold up a bank?"

Bill refused to give any information about the quarter. His only reply was to tell us all that he was going to buy a pickle every day that week. Envy spread.

Tuesday at lunch we waited again until the line shortened and then made our trip to the barrel. The line was not as long as it had been on Monday. We sat beneath our tree and savored the sour saltiness of our treat.

Wednesday was different. I held steadfast to my decision to make this the day I skipped. Bill joined the day's shorter line on his trip to the barrel. When he returned he munched contentedly while I drooled enviously in his direction. Bill did not share.

Thursday's trip was a joint effort again. The brine in the barrel was now low enough that I had to stand on the bottom step of the stool to reach far enough into it to retrieve a prize. Bill and I both paid for our pickles. We each had a nickel left for the last day of a glorious week.

We both wore corduroy pants to school. We each had two pairs, one brown and one blue. In the early days of the school year the pant legs swished as they passed each other. By the end of the year the knees would be worn smooth from our kneeling on them, and the pants would be shiny between the legs where they had rubbed together during the miles we walked.

Friday morning Bill put on his brown cords instead of his blue ones. We walked to school discussing how good a week we had had. We took the shortcut daily, looking for another quarter, but did not find one. When lunch arrived we walked directly to the lunch store. We were going to get our last pickle of the week to eat with our lunches. We left our brown bags under the tree, crossed the street, and entered the dark recesses of the lunch store. The line was really short on Friday. Bill walked right up to the barrel and reached in. He could barely touch the brine. He climbed up on the three-step stool and reached into the brine. He fished around, found a good-sized pickle, retrieved it, held up his prize, and stepped down from the stool. He reached into his pocket. The nickel was home in his blue cords.

Being smaller than Bill, I climbed to the top step of the stool and reached way down into the barrel. I reached into the salty liquor and felt for a pickle. I closed my hand over one just as Bill kicked the stool out from under my feet. I fell head first into the barrel. I knew I was going to drown. I couldn't swim. My head was under the brine and my feet were sticking out of the barrel. The owner, summoned by the screams of the other kids in line, came running to my aid. He grabbed me by my ankles and pulled me from the barrel. I was wet from the middle of my chest up. I smelled of vinegar and dill. I noticed Bill had left while I was being rescued.

When I reached the other side of the street, Bill was sitting under the tree eating his pickle. I arrived with my prize. The owner had toweled me off as best he could, and in order to quiet me he had given me a handful of licorice fish. I sat down and began eating my pickle. When I finished I reached into my pocket and took out a licorice fish.

"Where'd you get that?" Bill wanted to know.

"The owner gave them to me."

"How come?"

"I think he was sorry I fell into the barrel."

"You gonna share one with me?"

"Nope."

"Why not?"

"Because you kicked the stool out from under me and dunked me in the pickle barrel!" I said.

"I had to. I didn't have a nickel to pay for my pickle." Bill looked as if he were going to cry. "I had to do something to let me get out the door."

"Bill," I said, "guess what. I still have my nickel." I threw him a licorice fish. My teacher took one whiff of me after lunch and made me go home.

Chapter 12

That winter was a memorable one. The snows not only came early; they came deep. I had never seen so much snow. The snowplows turned down Roosevelt Av from Thirteenth East and pushed tremendous drifts to each side of the street. The drifts were taller than I was. Of course we walked down the tops of the snowdrifts. As we marched along the crusted top we found places that were not packed so well. Sometimes we sank in as deep as to the tops of our galoshes, other times to our waists. Once I dropped completely out of sight as I walked on a drift over a driveway.

Motorists cursed the snow; we applauded it with each new foot that fell. Roosevelt Av was so steep it became more and more difficult for cars to navigate it. Browning Av to the north had been designated as a sleigh-riding hill. The city put barricades at the top and bottom of the hill to protect sleigh riders from cars. Consequently no one used it as a sleigh-riding hill. It added a certain zest to compete with automobiles on Roosevelt Av.

Christmas came and went. My great gift from Santa Claus was a new sled. I broke my wrist and my sled handle on Christmas Day. The serious snows of winter continued to fall. My arm healed. More snow fell. They closed school one day, not because the kids couldn't get there, but because the teachers couldn't. I believe we had a hundred percent turnout of the kids at school. We all walked there to see if the school was really closed. It was.

The snow on the sides of the road was piled eight feet high. We could not see the road from our front window, only a snowdrift. The only breaks in these block-long snowdrifts appeared where brave souls had dug through the drifts to get their cars out of their driveways. Once they had dug out, the snowplow filled their driveways on the next pass.

We wired my sled handle back together, and Bill and I took turns riding down the hill. Often we rode double-decker, with Bill on the bottom, guiding. Sometimes Bill insisted that I ride on the bottom. It was uncomfortable having him on top, but at least I could steer. Bill's favorite trick was to pull my stocking cap down over my eyes, then roll off the sled, leaving me to crash into whatever lay ahead.

Trouble loomed on the horizon. The big kids, teenagers, in the neighborhood wanted to use the road for skiing. Roosevelt Av had about a foot of packed snow on the road itself. The plows had packed it for nearly eight weeks, and it approximated a ski run. These skiers wanted to ski straight down the road from Thirteenth East to Twelfth East. They didn't like us riding our sleds down the road for two reasons. First, we got in the way; and second, they claimed the runners on our sleds cut up the surface. While I will admit we got in the way, I believe it would have taken a heavily weighted spring-toothed plow to scratch the surface of that packed and frozen icing of snow on Roosevelt Av.

Bill became a pest. As a skier approached, he would scoot out of a driveway. Bill was never hit, but many of the skiers learned new gymnastics tricks avoiding him. At last they told Bill to stay out of the way or he would not be left in one piece. He believed them. Bill began looking for another place for us to ride my sled. We used Alan's backyard for some time. But the street was so much longer and better; Alan's place seemed too tame.

One Friday after school we were in our living room playing with my electric train. Bill was muttering about the injustice of the skiers, when he looked at the train coming out of the tunnel and said, "I've got it! We'll build a tunnel!"

Since I had no idea what he meant to do, or how he meant to do it, I merely nodded and kept the train going around the track. Bill quickly sprang to the phone and called the rest of the gang. "Bring your shovels and meet us on the corner of Thirteenth East," he commanded. Ten minutes later we were assembled.

Bill directed us to start digging a tunnel through the packed snow on the south side of Roosevelt Av. The tunnel was to be three feet wide and high enough for a sled and rider to go through. We were going to dig our tunnel clear down the road to Twelfth East. The only breaks in the tunnel would be at the driveways. This meant each segment of the tunnel would go between eighty and one hundred feet.

We began tunneling. The snow had been packed fairly well and the digging was tougher than we expected. After twenty minutes the five of us had managed to dig about five feet into the snowbank. Other problems arose. How do you pass snow out of a tunnel that size? We were lying flat on our stomachs on the bottom of the tunnel, trying to dig with a shovel straight in front of us and then trying to pass the snow back out of the tunnel. After ten feet of digging, the tunnel was starting to get dark. We had assumed that snow tunnels would be plenty light; after all, snow is white. We were also getting pretty cold. Discouragement set in. We began to complain. Bill suggested we stop for the day.

TV had come to Salt Lake City, and my father had bought a television set. Our set was an RCA with a twelve-inch screen. It was housed in a box the size of our Philco console radio. There were many knobs on the back of the TV set, and touching any one of them caused the picture to disappear. There were not many hours of programming available. Most of the time the only thing on the TV set was a test pattern. We liked to watch *Kukla, Fran, and Ollie* and Bill Boyd's Hopalong Cassidy cowboy movies. My father liked to watch the test pattern and the news. We tolerated the news because the weather was done by a hand puppet shaped like a crow. We hated the test pattern because my father used that opportunity to play with the knobs on the back of the television set. Often the picture disappeared.

After dinner my father was watching the news. A public service segment suggested that people should drain their water heaters twice a year to keep sediment from building up in the bottoms of them. My father suggested that we ought to do that sometime. Bill's eyes lit up. "We'll do it," he exclaimed.

My father looked at the two of us. "I don't think you two are big enough. The water is awfully hot and I don't want you two getting burned. I'll do it in the next couple of weeks."

"We can do it!" Bill said as a plan began to form in his head. "We'll be careful. You know how tired you are when you get home from driving all week."

"I'll do it in a couple of weeks," said my father as he turned back to watch the rest of the news.

The next morning Bill dragged me out to the garage. He climbed up on the picnic table and retrieved a garden hose from a hanger on the wall. The hose was cold and stiff and wanted to stay coiled. Bill retrieved the other hose stored there. "They'll be easier to use once the hot water's going through them," called out Bill as he dragged his coil of hose through the snow.

The rest of the gang were already working on the tunnel when Bill and I arrived with our two hoses. "We're gonna make this easier," said Bill. "We're gonna help all the people get the sentiment from their water heaters."

Bill marched up onto the Blakes' front porch. They lived in the house on the corner. He rang the doorbell. Mrs. Blake answered the door. "Did you see the news last night?" he began, forgetting that we owned one of only two TV sets on the whole street. "They told us to drain our water heaters."

Mrs. Blake shook her head. "I haven't heard anything about that." And she started to close the door.

"If we don't they could explode or something," said Bill. "We've just come to offer to drain yours for free!"

Mrs. Blake wavered. "I guess it can't hurt anything. What do you have to do?"

"We just have to hook this hose onto your water heater," said Bill, holding up the end of a hose. "It only takes a few minutes." Mrs. Blake looked worried. "We'll go to your basement door," said Bill as he stepped off her front porch.

Mrs. Blake opened her basement door, and Bill entered and screwed the end of the hose to the hose bib on her water heater. "Neil," Bill called, "when I give you the word, turn on the faucet." Neil took his place by the water heater. Bill unwound the stiff coil of hose, screwed on a nozzle, and aimed it into the opening of the snow tunnel. Alan and I stood by. "Tell Neil to turn on the water," Bill said to me.

Alan and I ran to the basement door. "Turn on the water."

Neil struggled with the faucet handle until finally a gush of hot water streamed from the hose.

Bill pulled the hose with him inside the tunnel and aimed the water against the wall of snow ahead of him. Snow melted and the tunnel enlarged. The hot water quickly melted a passage through the snowbank to the street. The melted snow water coursed out of the tunnel and ran down the side of the packed snow. After a few minutes the water running out of the hose cooled off. Bill had extended the tunnel another ten or twelve feet and had created several drain holes to the street. The cold water continued to melt the snow, although more slowly. After half an hour Bill called out of the tunnel. "Turn off the water." The message was passed to Neil, who managed to turn off the spigot. Bill emerged from the tunnel backward, thoroughly drenched. "It works," he said through chattering teeth.

Bill unscrewed the hose from Mrs. Blake's water heater. She seemed delighted we had not created a mess in her basement. Bill pulled the hose down the hill to the next house. By noon Bill had melted a tunnel halfway down the block. "I think this is long enough," he muttered through clenched, chattering teeth.

We helped put the hoses away before climbing back up the hill to the corner. The pants Bill was wearing had begun to freeze solid on his legs. He went home and changed clothes and returned with my sled. "Who's first?"

As Bill slid the sled into the tunnel opening, the handles barely missed the sides of the passageway. We all knelt down and peered into the tunnel. The clearance for our heads was questionable. "You get to go first, Bill. You made the tunnel," I said.

Bill lay down on the sled and inched himself forward into the tunnel with his mittened hands. The melted snow had frozen into a sheet of ice on the floor of the passageway. He started to slide down the tunnel. We ran and slipped down the street toward the first driveway. After a few steps we reached the frozen melt water at the side of the snowbank and down we went. Flat on our backs the four of us reached the first driveway opening at the same time the sled did. Bill was not on the sled. A moment later he slid into view. "The tunnel's too low," he said. "We'll just have to slide on our bellies. I just about hit my head." There was a red bump beginning to swell on his head.

Alan tried it next by sliding on his stomach through the tunnel. When he reached the first driveway opening he caught himself before he reentered the tunnel. He had had enough. Each of the rest of the gang tried sliding through the tunnel, and each one exited at the first opportunity. Bill called each of us chickens. "Let's see you go all the way down," we cried in unison. The gauntlet had been tossed.

Bill surveyed the tunnel. It ran from the corner past Alan's house, past our house, and past Mrs. MacElroy's house, and stopped on the far side of Fairbankses' driveway. He summoned his courage. We posted a sentry at each driveway. We dared Bill to slide all the way. He took one step toward the mouth of the tunnel and his feet slipped out from under him. He entered the tunnel on his back, feet first, and started to slide down the hill. He put his hands over his eyes and began to scream. He shot out of the tunnel at the first driveway, crossed it, and reentered. Ladd cheered, "He made it past me."

Bill cleared the next two driveways and started into the homestretch. At that moment an automobile emerged from Fairbankses' garage and backed down the driveway. The driver paused before entering the street. Bill shot out of the tunnel, under the running board of the car, and out the other side just as the car continued into the street. Bill crunched into the snowbank on the west side of the driveway. The front wheel of the car backed over the tassle on Bill's stocking cap. Snow began to fall.

The gang slipped and slid down the hill to Bill's aid. He stood up on shaking legs and watched the car drive down the road. We all went home.

It continued to snow all night. By noon the next day the snowplows had made their way down Roosevelt Av and filled in the driveways. We did not try to reclaim the tunnel.

Chapter 13

Finally the winter ended. It was followed by flooding. A flood went through the cemetery and relocated tombstones and grave markers. My Aunt Laura's house was just below the cemetery. Her basement was flooded and filled with mud and rocks. As they were cleaning it out, some bones were discovered. She was certain they had come from a grave. Actually they were from her neighbor's garbage can. They had eaten a leg of lamb the night before. Aunt Laura was never convinced of the leg-of-lamb story, however.

More memorable than the flooding was the completion of my Uncle Willard's house. He and Aunt Yuri packed the rest of their possessions and shipped them across the country from Maryland. Then they flew to Salt Lake. My mother and father took Bill and me to meet them at the airport. My uncle had grown shorter in the two years since I had last seen him. He said Bill and I had grown taller. After a brief reunion at the airport we loaded their baggage into the trunk of our trusty Chevrolet and started home. As we traveled from the airport toward downtown Salt Lake, my father asked, "Just where is your house, Willard?"

My uncle and aunt were in the backseat of the car with Bill between them. They turned and looked at each other. Finally my Uncle Willard said, "On Parley's Canyon Way."

My father looked puzzled. "Where's that?"

Again my uncle and aunt looked at each other. "East of the penitentiary."

This time my father and mother looked at each other. "How close to the penitentiary?" asked my mother.

"It's quite a ways from it," replied Uncle Willard.

"Let's go see," said my father.

Uncle Willard began to protest but realized we all would visit soon enough. Fifteen minutes later we were driving east on Twenty-first South past the front gates of the state penitentiary. As we reached the first road east of the prison, my Uncle Willard said, "Turn right." We turned right and drove along the fence line on the east side of the prison grounds. As we reached the first intersection, my uncle said, "Turn left." There stood a brand-new two-story house barely half a block from the prison grounds. Even my Aunt Yuri looked shocked.

We pulled into the driveway, and my uncle got out of the car and unlocked the front door. It was a lovely home. Bill's bedroom was on the second floor. His window looked straight west at the penitentiary. "I wonder," he mused, "what would happen if we launched a cherry bomb into the prison yard late some night." During the next decade we discovered the answer to that question, along with many others yet unformulated.

Bill moved into his new home during the next week. The spring rains were coming to a halt. Trustees were planting corn in the prison garden just west of Bill's house. My Aunt Yuri forbade us from going anywhere near the barbed-wire fence. Bill, of course, discovered that his ball often bounced toward the fence, and, in time, he became friends with several of the prisoners.

Although I saw Bill every day at school, he began developing new friends near his new house. Mark Pierce had moved in across the street six months before Bill moved into his new place. Mark and Bill became fast friends. I was two years younger and was considered a nuisance.

Occasionally Bill spent the night at my house. The gang no longer accepted him as leader, and his suggestions were often rejected. His visits became fewer and fewer. At the end of the schoolyear he left Emerson and transferred to Uinta Elementary. Another strand of our intertwined lives was broken.

No Tarzan ropes hung from the trees. The hut was becoming too small to accommodate the four members of the gang at one time. Slats split, fell off, and were not replaced.

Halloween approached, and the gang considered replaying the events from two years before; however, the memories of punishment were still too vivid. We decided we were not too old to go trick-or-treating.

The first flakes of snow brought memories of sleighs, skis, and tunnels . . . and Bill; but with each passing season the memories dimmed. Although my mother had been the one who agreed to let Bill live with us, she seemed happy that he was now in his own home. Often she commented that she hoped I hadn't been damaged for life. Sometimes, while sitting in her favorite chair, she'd exhale a mighty sigh, shake her head, and whisper, "Bill."

And at that moment I'd look out our front window at the hut in the tree in the woods, and smile.

About the Author

Richard M. Siddoway was raised in Salt Lake City, Utah. He received his bachelor's degree from the University of Utah and his master's degree in instructional systems and learning resources from the same institution. A professional educator for over thirty years, he is currently the director of the Electronic High School for the State of Utah and represents his district in the Utah State Legislature. He is the author of the nationally best-selling book *The Christmas Wish,* as well as *Twelve Tales of Christmas, Mom—and Other Great Women I've Known,* and *Habits of the Heart.*

The author and his wife, the former Geri Hendrickson, had six children prior to her untimely death from cancer. He has since married the former Janice Spires, and they have a combined family of eight children.